John W. May

Inside the Bar

And other Occasional Poems

John W. May

Inside the Bar
And other Occasional Poems

ISBN/EAN: 9783744770491

Printed in Europe, USA, Canada, Australia, Japan

Cover: Foto ©Andreas Hilbeck / pixelio.de

More available books at **www.hansebooks.com**

TRANSITION SCENE.

"From dusty law-books what an awful stride
To that bright seat the beaming Muse beside!"

p. 94.

INSIDE THE BAR

AND

OTHER OCCASIONAL POEMS

BY

JOHN W. MAY.

"Aut insanit homo, aut versus facit."—HORACE.

PORTLAND, ME.:
HOYT, FOGG & DONHAM.
1884.

JOURNAL PRESS, LEWISTON, ME.

AUBURN, ME., Feb. 1, 1884.

BROTHER MAY:

As Secretary of the Androscoggin Bar Association I forward you herewith a copy of Resolutions, requesting the publication of your poems.

These Resolutions were offered by Hon. George C. Wing, and were adopted by unanimous vote of the Association at a meeting held at the Court-House, Jan. 16, 1884.

I feel that I express the wish of the Association when I request your early action in accordance with the same.

Sincerely Yours,

H. W. OAKES,

Secretary.

JOHN W. MAY, ESQ., Auburn, Me.

RESOLUTIONS.

Whereas, Brother JOHN W. MAY has at different times in the past composed a large number of poems on different topics, particularly the Androscoggin Bar, its members and practice, some of which have been published, and all of which have given pleasure to the Bar and afforded satisfaction to its members, therefore

Resolved, That it is the wish of the Bar that Bro. MAY be requested to collect his several poetical effusions and cause the same to be published in book form, to the end that they may be preserved and secured to the Bar and to his many friends, who highly appreciate not only his worth as a man, his ability and integrity as a counselor at law, but his rare and happy gift as a poet.

A true copy.

ATTEST:

H. W. OAKES,

Secretary.

To the Androscoggin Bar Association, by whose complimentary vote these waifs have been referred to with a request for collection and preservation, and for the amusement and entertainment of whose members most of them were originally written,—the same having been the work of leisure hours, and suggested, to a large extent, by observations and incidents in Court, and by achievements and characteristics of individual members of the Association, and intended only for the day and the occasion,—this volume is respectfully inscribed by one of their number, who is under obligations to them for many favors and courtesies, and whose aspirations in this department of *belles-lettres*, will be sufficiently gratified if he has contributed something in his way to their enjoyment.

J. W. M.

Lewiston, August, 1884.

TABLE OF CONTENTS.

— ·· —

OCCASIONAL POEMS.

PREFACE.

It is perhaps quite unnecessary to make any remarks, explanations, or apologies to accompany the publication of such "effusions" as these. They were written at different times, more for amusement and the entertainment of the writer's associates at the Bar, than with any view to their collection and publication. In responding to the flattering request of our Association, the purpose has been, so far as practicable, to prepare a book which, it is hoped, may commend itself to the legal profession in Maine, and at the same time present some attractions to the public at large. I am aware that its interest is to a considerable extent local, and also, that it contains many personalities: the latter however, I believe it is well understood, were all conceived in good nature and have been used with the kindest intentions. If the volume serves as an occasional cordial to the legal fraternity who have asked its publication, its leading purpose will be accomplished.

In reference to the illustrations, I would say, the idea was an after-thought. It was the opinion of some of my brethren of the Bar, that several of the poems were susceptible of illustration, and that additional interest would be given to the book if suitable illustrations could be obtained. I desire to acknowledge my obligations to the artist, Mr. D. D. Coombs of Auburn, for the satisfactory manner in which he has executed his part of the work.

J. W. M.

Lewiston, Me., August, 1884.

INSIDE THE BAR.

GRAVE DOUBTS.

There's a measly distemper which sometimes afflicts
Gentlemen of the bar and advice interdicts:
It defieth the doctors, all physic it scouts;
To-day it is on me,—a touch of grave doubts.

Have you never had 'em, O brothers, declare,—
When you've wrestled and tugged till about to despair,
With some tough old conundrum too stubborn to yield
To the logic incisive which you and I wield?

Have you never heard the low, guttural sound
That proceeds from the depths when one struggles pro-
    found
With great arguments *pro* and great arguments *con*,
Till he gropes in the cobwebs perplexed and undone?

Shall I give it up, when the burgher of fame,
The great Wouter Van Twiller, so noted became
For his marvelous skill at revolving in mind,
And never deciding the issue defined?

Nil, nil desperandum! Aut gloria, aut nil!
If I keep from you, brothers, these treasures until
Some spirit doth prompt me to launch 'em abroad,
You'll lose all the salad, and I the reward.

1

Come out from your pigeon-holes, dainties, come here!
All soiled with the dust and unfit to appear :—
Let me brush off the mould and the dingy mildew ;
Let me do up the budget, fresh, shiny, and new.

Ah! when I am up on the high rounds of fame,
I'll decide upon something, though doubting the same ;
Meantime let me ponder and smoke if I crave,
And keep up the battle with doubts that are grave.

If perchance the low guttural sound you should hear,
Then be sure, in the depths, there's a tussle severe ;
That some problem of doubt on the hip has got hold
And hangs fire as it did with the burgher of old.

SETH SAMPSON, ESQ.

ANDROSCOGGIN, SS.:

OR THE MYSTERIES AND EMOLUMENTS OF THE LAW EXPLAINED.

Androscoggin, ss.! a significant phrase,
Interpreted here in divers queer ways:
Not a writ, a return, or a record is made,
But *Androscoggin, ss.* is out on parade.
Now the lawyers, and sheriffs, and clerk of the courts
All know the deep meaning this law phrase imports;
But the vulgar plebeians, they never could guess
The full force of the words, *Androscoggin, ss.*

Androscoggin, indeed, is the bailiwick's name;
SS. is the sticker, what meaneth the same?
Videlicet, say some,—*soft soder, soft soap;*—
Such sneer at the law as some sneer at the Pope,
Deriding its weightier matters instead of
The mint and the anise and cumin we've read of.
Others wiser, assert with more serious intent,
Seth Sampson, Esquire, is the man who is meant;—
Seth Sampson who sits 'tween the bench and the bar,
And hearkens to catch every lisp of the law,
And feeds on such fodder, though he never grows fat,
But leaner and lanker, more sharp and all that,—
Till he looks like some genius judicial let loose
From a case of old law books grown dingy with use,
All pickled and dried in the essence of law,
And as full of sharp points as the brief that you draw.
With his long gray hair and his antique clothes,
And his ponderous *specs* a-straddle his nose,

And his *calf-skin* vest so odd you would laugh
At the ancient volume thus bound in calf,—
Seth Sampson, they say, is the phantom ss.;
Look out for his clutches, you rogues who transgress.

In the trial of cases called civil, 'tis true,
Androscoggin, ss. but proclaims the " *venue* ";
While in criminal causes, by legal intent,
Both " *venue* " and the " *populi salus* " are meant.
The majesty stern of the county at large
Stands up and speaks out in the criminal charge ;
Making burglars, and thieves, and assassins and rakes
Pay the penalties due for their mischief's mistakes.
Androscoggin, ss. is a summons of fear
When it reaches the precincts of pea-nuts and beer,
Disturbing the hucksters and leaving withal
A margin for profits exceedingly small.

Eliza McM. was most grievously poor ;
Androscoggin, ss. had been 'round to her door
In the person of two or three bright button chaps,
Whose call was unwelcome and boded mishaps.
High words had been heard in Eliza's abode ;
Some guests had gone forth with too much of a load,
And the scent of " *R. G.*," as the button chaps swore,
Told a tale of the " *slewed* " at Eliza's own door.
Now these button chaps bolted right into her house,
And Eliza showed fight which raised a great touse ;—
They looked in the cupboards and smelled of the cans ;
She whacked a big bottle right out of their han's
With a blow of the poker, and smash on the floor,
Went the " *little cold water* " she'd kept in her store.
They smelled of the bottles and tumblers and jugs,
They smelled of the tea-cups and saucers and mugs,

And they searched for a smell amid storms of abuse,
But never smelled " *water* " at all in the house.

Androscoggin, *ss.* called Eliza in court
On a charge which both *keeping* and *sale* did import,
And Eliza arraigned faltered faint in distress,—
" *Not guilty yer honor, it's a lie of* ss."
" Are you ready for trial, have you counsel engaged?"
Said the judge to Eliza, her grief unassuaged :
" *No counsel your honor; I am too poor, sir, to pay*
Any lawyer to help me." Here fainted away
The poor, trembling Eliza, till, touched by her grief,
The judge assigned counsel, which brought some relief.
But the jury, despite all the counsel could do,
Said : " *Guilty of keeping and selling it too.*"
And the judge imposed sentence of hundreds and cost,
Or jail for long months in which profits are lost,—
A terrible doom for poor 'Liza McM.,
Convicted, condemned, *in persona*, *in rem*.

But she had a big pocket down deep in her dress ;
She went down to its bottom in this her distress
And she brought up a wad of the greenbacks and paid
Every cent of the fine and the costs, and she said :
" *Ye talked well for me, lawyer; it grieves me to say*
I'm too poor for your excellent talking to pay;
I've but fifty cents left—take that, sir, and when
The button chaps plague me,—I'll want ye again."
Here she sobbed with a sob of more startling distress,
And she cursed the old cove, *Androscoggin*, *ss.*

In brief (for in fact, I'm but writing a *brief*,)
Androscoggin, *ss.* is an arrant old thief ;
He plundered Eliza, a destitute woman,
And treated her, too, in a way most inhuman ;

He took all her profits and never said grace ;
He left for the lawyer who pleaded her case
But a fifty-cent scrip, which was meaner than dirt.
Now I join with Eliza and boldly assert.
(And I rise with authorities strong to sustain
The point that I make and now mean to maintain,)
That of all the old hogs that root 'round in the street,
Androscoggin, *ss.* is the meanest you meet ;
For he grabs for the whole with a merciless grip,
Leaving scarce for the lawyer a fifty-cent scrip.

Here I close in the faith I have made out a case ;
Shall I hear a " *non constat* " now flung in my face?
The jury may judge and a verdict express.
I have argued my cause, *Androscoggin*, *ss.*,
State of Maine, if you please, *versus 'Liza McM.* :
Androscoggin, *ss.* made the grab, sir, *in rem.*

THE PRICE OF THE PIG.

[LEWISTON MUNICIPAL COURT, 1872. KNOWLTON, J., PRESIDING.]

There was a man whose name was H.,
  Lived o'er in Auburn town ;
He had two pigs, and each was worth
  A "V" or more, cash down.

Another man whose name was V.,
  Of that same Auburn town,
For winter's pork a pig would buy,
  Fat, kill, and then salt down.

The first he was a farmer man,
  A butcher, too, by trade ;
The other was a mason man
  And bricks in mortar laid.

"Now, hang it," saith the mason man,
  "I'll have a pig 'twill thrive ;
Snug-boned, with moderate breadth of beam,
  And weight, say, seventy-five.

"I'll have a beauty of a pig,
  As sure's my name is V."
"Ha, ha," he laughed for very joy,
  So fond of pigs was he.

He saw those pigs scarce four months old,
    Of farmer H., the pride,
And one he liked,—he took a week
    To ponder and decide.

One morning at his mason work,
    Some fearful pork might rise,
He saw the farmer riding by,
    And hailed him in this wise :

" Say, do you know where I can buy
    A good spring pig, 'twill weigh
Some seventy-five or hundred pounds?
    I want to buy to-day."

" Don't b'lieve I do," quoth farmer H.,
    " But there's those pigs of mine ;
Six dollars, you can have your choice,
    A bargain 'tis in swine."

" Too small, too small," quoth mason V.,
    " Now I don't want to buy
A pig that's under seventy-five,
    Like those in your pig-sty."

" Hout, tout !" quoth farmer H., " I judge
    The row-back pig will weigh
Full sixty pounds." " Nonsense !" said V.,—
    " Small pork such price to pay."

" Give me six dollars for that pig,"
    Rejoined the farmer, then,
" And I will straightway bring him o'er
    And leave him in your pen."

" You call him sixty?—well," said V.,
　" Deliver him, 'tis a trade ; "
V. chuckled in his sleeve to think
　What bargain he had made.

Home from his mason work at night
　He went with spirits high,
And in his own peculiar pen
　The row-back met his eye.

" Faith, he don't weigh no seventy-five,
　Nor sixty pounds, I *vum!*
Wife, bring the steelyards,—well, I know
　That we've been cheated some."

Over into that pen he leaped,
　Full lively on his taps ;
He caught that little, gentle pig,
　And slung him up in straps.

And hung him on the steelyard hook,
　And poised him in the air—
Squealing and kicking all his might,
　So fearful was the scare.

The steelyard arm he then brought down,
　And balanced with the weight ;
When, lo ! the startling fact appeared,
　The pig weighed forty-eight.

" I swan," said V., " that's mean enough ;
　I vow I'll never pay ;
The man may go to H–alifax,
　Who'll use me in that way."

" **Four** dollars is the most I'll pay ;—
   Wife you remember that ;
We'll keep the pig and feed him well,
   And kill him when he's fat."

A month or more elapsed before
   H. called for dollars six ;
V. swore he'd never pay but **four**,
   As long as he laid bricks.

Now, here sprung up a direful **feud,**
   About the pig and pay ;
And soon in court as litigants,
   Each party had his day.

And lawyers haggled in **the case,**
   And argued *pro* and *con ;*
The hash was settled **by the judge,**
   The plaintiff **'twas who won.**

Alas, for V.'s scant winter's pork,
   Full **dear** at dollars **six ;**
It cost him over twenty-five,
   Hard earned **at laying bricks.**

And beans with pork he **only** had,
   Not twice but once a week,—
A hardship of the direst kind,
   Of which I grieve to speak.

And here this doleful ballad ends,
   Tho' half **remains untold ;**
The lawsuit was a tougher **bill**
   Than twenty pigs thus sold.

The confidence of mason V.
　　In farmer II. is gone ;
But not his confidence in pork,
　　Be lawsuits lost or won.

Oftimes in dreams at night he sees,
　　Hung dangling in the air,
A kicking pig, whose dismal cries,
　　Say : " Mason man, beware ! "

Beware of lawsuits on a pig,
　　They bring the pork too high ;
Lay bricks and always pay the bill,
　　When e'er a pig you buy.

Avoid a suit and save the cost,
　　For it will buy much pork ;
Beans, you can have them twice a week,—
　　Backbone for mason work.

Now let this tale a lesson be,
　　To every willful man ;
Buy corn instead of law for pigs
　　'Tis far the wiser plan.

'Twill yield more pork, less trouble, too ;
　　And those infernal dreams
Of dangling, kicking, squealing pigs
　　Will cause no nightmare screams.

Then pleasantly his days will pass,
　　His barrel aye be full ;
The juicy bean-pot add its cheer,
　　And ne'er his heart sing dool.

THE STORY TELLER.

"OWED" TO WING.

[S. J. Court, Sept. T., 1872.   Walton, J., Presiding.]

Oh, Wing, you are a "*phunny phellow*,"
Your stories fairly make me bellow:
You told some rippers 'tother night
At the DeWitt,—I laughed outright;
So loud indeed my laughter rung,
Two buttons from my waistbands sprung.

Say, Wing, you genius, how did you
This knack acquire? Pray tell us, do?
Was it in story-telling school
You learned the art by rote and rule,
Or was it born within your brain?
Come, Wing, my chap, this thing explain.

Byron and Shelley, Burns and Hood
The art of verse all understood,
And Dr. Samuel Johnson, he
Sang big frog's chant to little frog-ee.
But when the story part comes in,
With you, O Wing, they can't begin.

How Frye and Ludden, Record, Wright,
Did shake their sides with huge delight,
And Cotton, too, did roar and surge
As loud as in a jury splurge;
And e'en that upright man, Judge Luce,
Marveled like child at Mother Goose!

'Twas late that night when I got home,
The "*wee sma' hours*" indeed had come:
I laid me down and tried to sleep,
But, whew! your stories tough did keep
High carnival, —I was not drunk,
Though thrice I heard you say: "*Ker-dunk.*"

I tell you, Wing, you ought to shine!
Just treasure up your stories fine
And put 'em in a book all told:
Hot cakes for lawyers, young and old,
Nuts, raisins, sweetmeats, charlotte-russe,
Cream cake or jelly, as you choose.

I'll buy one of the books and so
Will Frye and Ludden, Record too.
And Cornish, Pulsifer and Frost,
And all the rest. Don't mind the cost.
Let Stanwood bind 'em with a clasp,
And keep 'em from the vulgar grasp.

And, Wing, one word before I close,—
Whene'er you ventilate your views
Before the jury or the judge,
If argument should fail, don't budge:
Your fiddle has another string,
You'll take 'em with a story, Wing.

A PÆAN FOR THE CITY.

[JANUARY 1, 1872.]

The city expands. Do you see how it grows,
And what mighty proportions its suburbs disclose?
The city, I say,—and I speak it with pride,—
Though I'm o'er the bridge, just a little outside.
The city's a wonder! Go out if you will,
Beyond brick-kilns and shanties, the city's there still;
I defy you to tell, passing out, sir, or in,
Where the city doth stop, and the country begin.

For a child of ten years, the city's a thing
Decidedly big—*et ergo*, I sing:
Now, Muse, flap your wings like a brisk chanticleer
And crow for the city a *lusty new year*.

There were cities of old demolished by fire,
Gomorrah and Sodom,—there were Sidon and Tyre,
Both places of note, which grew very fast,
But their glory burned out like a candle at last;
There was great Babylon, sir, a very fast town,
With its gardens hung high, but they had to come down.
Now what is the moral? The moral is plain:
City folks of their city ought not to be vain;
And I mention these things just to show that I am

2

Aware of the fact that **town pride is a sham.**
Brick and mortar do **much for a town, it is true:**
So do fat corporations, and water-power, **too:**
Banks. colleges, saw-mills and **school-marms** and stores.
And high-steepled churches **no townsman** ignores.
Smart men and fair ladies, bright **boys, sir, and** girls,
With their lustrous, dark eyes and luxuriant curls,
And cheeks like a plum, **which one hankers** to taste.
(Keep steady, O Muse, and **your** balance well braced.)
Are things which, by jingo, I never **can** see
Without dipping my **pen for** a slight *jeu d'esprit.*
So I **crack** for this city, which excels in all these :
You may find as much fault with my rhyme as **you please,**
And say, better hush **up** lest mischief betide
The chap o'er the bridge, **just a little outside.**

Look at Lisbon Street now, magnificent **mart**
Of fabrics and **notions and rare things of** art!
Where a suit, or a picture, or paper of corn
You can buy with your money, sir, sure as your born ;
Where the dry goods and fancy **make** show **till** one **stares**
As he would **if he strolled** through the Turkish bazars ;
Where the fashions are out, where the horses are **fast,**
And the **livery of** town dashes fearfully past ;
Where the **barbers'** poles shine, **and** they shave **you so**
          snug,—
Those knights of **the razors, the brush and the mug,—**
And they shave you so neat, and **they** smile **when they're**
          paid,
As blandly as shavers who shave on a trade.
Look **at Lisbon Street, sir ! Pray,** where is its match?
It begins **at** a church **and it ends in "** *the patch,*"
The patch where p–ratees and babies are raised
In bountiful crops,—let the good Lord be praised !

Hail, *Linkin Street*, hail! Thou region where dwells
A vast combination of undefined smells,
Which riot abroad on a hot summer's day,
And the cold breath of winter scarce keeps them at bay.
Walk down, if you please, through that long thoroughfare,
And see what a mixture doth congregate there:
Hear the *parlez vous* chat, and the *broguers* declaim,—
Sure, *Linkin Street's* something, sir, more than a name!
There's business done there, as every one knows,
Aside from the drunks and the jolly old rows;
There are shops where the windows show candy and cake,
And holes in the ground where there's "*suthin' to take*";
For Eliza keeps there, the poor, destitute woman,
Whom the button chaps plagued and treated inhuman.
With its rabbles and rows, and confusion of tongues,
To *Linkin Street*, sir, there's a history belongs;
And *Patrick* and *Bridget*, *Jean Baptiste* and all
Make it thrive like an ant-hill in sunshine and squall.
From the gas works below, to the store of E. Keen,
Pigs, puppies, and urchins enliven the scene;
And the hubbub that's raised by young *Erin-go-bragh*,
Resounds through the length of the grand *Boulevard*.

There's another place, too, once headquarters, and still
A place of some note, called "*under the hill*";
Which rejoices in Keen and the noted Sam Hicks,
Who's *at home*, sir, and up to his famous old tricks.
Buy your beef, sir, of Keen, and your stews, sir, of Sam;
You'll be sure to grow fat and be happy's a clam.
Get a lounge in at Conant's and stretch yourself out,
And laugh at old sinners who growl with the gout:
Buy a rifle at Nason's and shoot at a mark,
Buy a cook stove of Goss and in cooking embark,—
Pay your bills when you buy, if you don't you'll get
    hit,—

There's a lawyer down there who sometimes makes a **writ**,
And follows delinquents up with a sharp stick,
With a very sharp point,—and **I've known it to prick.**
The lawyer **keeps sober,—he's never** *a brick.*

Whew! I'm quite out of breath. Guess here I'll alight,
And take Pegasus in and give him a bite.
But I'll breathe, ere I stop, a godspeed for the town,
And the blast of trumpet, I think, should be blown.
Go on, O smart city! Your banners fling out!
Revolve all your spindles and spindle it out!
If we only survive and don't burst with this strain,
Next year, by the Moses! we'll pæan again
And give a big lift for the city,—Who knows?—
Hush, now! It is time that this pæan should close.

THE HIGH HAND OF THE LAW.

LINES TO THE CLIPPER.

ON THE EVENING OF ARREST, NOV. 8, 1873.

[The *Auburn Clipper*, published a few years ago in Auburn, was styled by some of its contemporaries, " *The Free Lance in Journalism*." It was conducted with spirit and ability and scored many good points in its locals; but its personalities were carried to such an extreme that it soon got into trouble. The language and epithets it used in reference to the Judge of the Lewiston Municipal Court were so outrageous that the editors were summoned to answer for contempt and punished by fine and imprisonment.]

Audacious, spicy little *Clipper*,
Insulting, mischievous, yet chipper!
I fear ye took a double nipper
      Last Monday morn,
Such as Eliza's old quart dipper
      Was wont to turn.

What makes ye pitch into 'em so,
An' then your horn defiant blow?
Ye should be spanked and taught to know
      Some better manners:
Ye've no respec' for high or low,
      Not e'en for *Tanners*.

Folks' backs is up. I hear they've got
A warrant out all hissing hot,
An' ta'en ye o'er at lively trot
      To see the Judge,
Who for yer *sass* as like as not
      Owes ye a grudge.

I hear his Honor bound ye o'er
To answer,—bonds a half a score
O' thousand dollars,—so no more
      Yer pizen slang
Ye'll sling contemptuous at his door,—
      I guess ye'll hang;

Or else go o'er awhile to tarry
Wi' Tom, the "City Missionary";
He takes such pupils temporary,
    An' on long time,
But 'lows no swearin', drinkin' sherry,
    Nor slingin' slime.

Yer sins they say are grievous many:
Ye never gather up a penny
But wi' a dose o' salts and senna,
    Ye go for some on',
Who ne'er perchance has harmed ye any,
    An' dare him come on.

Last summer when the chivalry
Marched down by moonlight to the sea,
Ye turned yer guns on Cap'n P.,
    Quite unrefined,
An' limbered his artillery
    "*In the rear behind.*"

Last month ye had a jag for Cheney;
I must confess I thought ye spleeny
To talk so rude. What did ye mean, ha?
    Those Baptist fellers,
They'll serve ye with a fresh subpœna,
    You and yer sellers.

An' now on Gov'nors, Congressmen,
The best folks of the upper ten,
An' e'en the *Journal's* busy pen,
    What writes reports,
Ye empty slops from your vile den,
    All kinds and sorts.

' Twas you, not Kenway, drew *the plan*
About the affair up Switzerlan',
An' passed it to the *Journal* man
  To copy gratis:
But he, chaste man, the *Clipper's* plan
  Disdained to notice.

I 'spect he thought that " *interest weird*,"
To which his columns had appeared
To pander, had played out,—I feared
  The gypsy camp
Part of the story was *too* **weird**,
  E'er to revamp.

Now, *Clipper*, as it's gettin' late,
I will no more expostulate;
I doubt if any lawyer's pate
  Can here unravel
What is to be your legal fate,
  What road you'll travel;

I hopes they will not snuff ye out,
Or put yer wits to total rout:
Abate some o' yer rank sour-krout
  An' then ye'll go it,
An' patrons have enough, no doubt,
  Perhaps a poet.

Put in the ginger and the spice,—
(I charge ye naught for this advice,)
Ye well are worth yer sellin' price,
  Ye little ripper,
Ye'll lick 'em all—heed my advice,—
  Two cents a *Clipper!*

THE DOG THAT BIT McFINNIHADDIE.

Who would not swear, nor take it back,
Tho' at him howled the wolfish pack?
The miscreant cur that bites a *Mac*
Shall die by swift shillalah whack,
   Or pistol shot, McFinnihaddie.

No matter whether, big or small,
He strays from Breen's or Brophy's stall,
Him let policemen prompt o'erhaul:
He'd better be no dog at all
   Than bite the boy, McFinnihaddie.

Of all the scabby curs that prowl
On Lincoln Street, an' hungry howl
An' snap at urchins, pigs, an' fowl,—
Not one shall live, upon my soul,
   To bite the blood, McFinnihaddie.

The murthering scamp, they killed him dead;
The gamins shouted when he bled.
He bit young *Mac:* an' now 'tis said
The jury have a poultice spread
   To heal the wound, McFinnihaddie.

A dollar for each pound he weighed
Was doubled; an' when this is paid,
Then reparation will be made,
An' all the pain will be allayed,
   That stirred the blood, McFinnihaddie.

My faith! May be the price is cheap!
(Though Breen I fear will count it steep,)
I think if well-bred dogs, that sleep
On downy rugs, a court should keep,
          An' try the case, McFinnihaddie ;

The verdict they would render back
Would be : No dog, or white or black,
That bites a boy an' then makes track,
An' 'scapes the marshal's pistol crack,
          Shall dwell with men, McFinnihaddie :

But homeless he shall prowl abroad,
A miscreant of the outlawed horde,
An' his dead head shall bring reward ;
An' men shall dock his caudal cord
          Close to his ears, McFinnihaddie.

Alas for Breen! With him all's up,—
Attached in law and dead his pup,
When he at night sits down to sup
There's naught but trouble in his cup ;
          He's woful down, McFinnihaddie.

For costs an' damage, items long,
Full high, full dear, full steep an' strong,
He's got to foot,—an' for *his* wrong
Nobody cares a beggar's song.
          Who's bit the worse, McFinnihaddie?

THE ORIGINAL CHARGE.

THE BULL CASE.

[Cotton for Plf.   Record for Deft.]

"Oh, J. B. Cotton! Say what you should do
If you were a woman, hystericky, too,
And a rampant bull made a dive at you?

"Should you holler an' scream with vigor intense;
Should you take to your heels, or take to the fence
And over it go an' battle him thence?

"Suppose the critter all unconfined
Should level his horn at you behind,—
You, a woman to fidgets inclined?

" Suppose he should bellow an' lash his tail,
An' charge on the fence till the topmost rail
Fell over on you, low squat an' pale ;

" Screaming an' crying for help in vain,
Tortured with fear an' tortured with pain,
What should you do, I ask again?

" You know that a woman so sensitive born,
Can't cope with a monster having a horn
An' threatening to gore her all forlorn.

" You know 'tis unsafe, outrageous an' wrong
To let such a Bashan, so savage an' strong,
Break loose an' bellow the streets along.

" You know, when his firey eyeballs glare
And his tail goes up, he's a terrible scare
To a sensitive woman so apt to despair.

" Now these are the facts explicit, precise ;
I ask for the law an' care not for the price.
Pray give me the best o' your legal advice."

" Good madam, I think 'twas *malice* **prepense**
In the bull, a case of damage immense,
To which there can be no valid defense.

" The owner or keeper is clearly at fault ;
See Blackstone or Chitty, title, Assault.
The case is as clear as a kick from a colt."

But alas for opinions an' legal advice !
Good cases, when tried an' argued so nice,
Are oftentimes lost by subtle device.

The jury, on weighing the evidence full,
Concluded somehow, by a pull o' the wool,
The woman it was that inveigled the bull.

MORAL.

So J. B. Cotton, my **friend, I fail**
To discover the reason you didn't **prevail,**
Unless 'twas taking the bull by **the tail.**

Next time you tackle the **Unicorn,**
Though he bellow an' **blaze** like **a demon hell-born,**
Don't grab for his tail,—take hold **of his horn.**

THE CANINE FERTILIZER.

—

[A new agricultural contrivance once on exhibition at J. G. Cook's drug store in Lewiston. The machine is charged with a cartridge and set in operation by the application of a lighted match. The *modus operandi* may be gathered from these lines :]

I laughed all day, an' when abed
I still kept laughin', an' I said:
That little dog there made o' lead,
   Curled o'er his haunches,
Drops his fertility unspread,
   Small avalanches.

Just now I thought,—Faith, he is done ;
Now he will gather up an' run,
An' wag his tail an' ha' some fun,—
   But, Moses' mother !
Ere I could wink, he straight begun
   To do another.

An' such a string ! Lord, keep my tongue
From tellin' lies an' sayin' wrong !
I would na' dare to say how long,
   I did na' measure,
But guess 'twould reach if it were strong,
   Up to the azure.

An' then he heaped so fast his pile,
In such a funny, off-han' style,
It seem'd that inside out the while
   The scamp was turnin',
An' which was dog, an' which was pile,
   'Twas hard discernin'.

Oh, Shucks! He's hoaxin' us, said I:
For no lank pup beneath the sky,
Since days o' miracles went by,
          No bigger 'n that one,
Could string it thus. 'Twould fetch a sigh
          From any fat one.

A regular Ah Sin he is.—
I'd like to know what makes his phiz
So pensive,—doin' such a biz:
          What feeds the hopper
To that small grinding mill o' his,
          An' where's the stopper?

Oh, I have seen beside the street
Vile curs the effort oft repeat
An' nothin' do but scrape their feet,
          An' sometimes bark it,—
I've wished the doctor'd come an' treat
          'Em with cathartic.

An' I've seen boys lock fingers, too,
An' pull for dogs, to help 'em thro'
In such dilemma, when I knew
          Those heartless boys
Made mockery 'o the dog's ado,
          Wi' shout an' noise.

But this 'ere small on' asks no help.
An' never yet since he was whelp
Did make a fuss an' whine an' skelp
          Behind the barn,
But braces up without a yelp
          An', lo, his yarn!

OBITER DICTA.

[DEC. 7, 1872.]

In these short days. when calls are few
And lawyers have not much to do,
While briefs are finished and the Court
In chambers tries your case of tort,—
Whose business if one pokes aside
The sheep-skin volumes, worn and dried,
And from his table sweeps the dirt,
And takes in rhyme a little flirt?

The outside world moves on : and why,
When other nags are stirring spry,
Why should not Pegasus come out
And whisk his long, white tail about?
Let not the jockeys scoff at him ;—
He goes it sometimes with a vim,
Nor loses tail, nor hair, nor hide,
'Tho' on a Tam O'Shanter's ride.

Behold how gorgeous are the styles!
Triumphant millinery smiles
And flaunts the streets full-plumed to-day.
Whose wife is that, so dashing gay,
That's shopping fearless thro' the town,
Nor cares a fig for husband's frown?
What fur-trimm'd, feathery maidens those
Like snow-birds on the wintry snows?

3

O my! the nobby seal-skin hats!
What perfect little Ararats,
That tower above the flood o' trash
Which cheap folks buy to make a dash!
Ho, sable, mink, and fitch, get out!
You only make the fair ones pout,
When royal seal skin rules *so high;—*
Ask Getchell if you think I lie.

The city's Temple is complete,
A monument that's hard to beat;
And dedicated all so grand,—
O townsman, let your pride expand!
" *Exegi monumentum æ-*
Re perennius! " Did you see
The elephant inside the ring
Dancing last night the Highland fling?

Go down, you sorehead, double quick,
And see your pile o' hard-burnt brick;
Look 'round awhile, look up the sky,—
Is it a planet meets your eye,
Or streaming meteor all ablaze?
Put on your spec's and steadfast gaze:
You mutton head! Why, don't you know
That is the steeple glistens so?

Shake hands with a policeman now;
Tell him you come to see the show;
Tell him you'd like to just walk in
And thro' the Temple, then out ag'in.
Give him a rag or two o' scrip:
He'll take you then aboard the ship
And thro' the halls and all about,—
The sights will make your eyes stick out.

Compare this proud, imperial day
With days not long since passed away,—
Days remembered by Doctor G.,
When woods were here as well as he;
And hunters set their fox-traps where
The Doctor rocks in his easy chair.
" *Historical fact!*" The Doctor said;
" *Tho' most who know it now are dead.*"

" *Oh, Doctor G.! If, as you tell,*
The traps were set there where you dwell,"
Said Col. B., " *I pray you avow,*
What hinders settin' the traps there now?
Was't ever a fox the hunters caught?"
To which the Doctor rejoined in short:
" *I spoke of traps, and not of game;*
Impertinent Col., forshame, forshame!"

Scud home now, Pegasus, prancing fleet,
With white tail whisking thro' the street,
Scud 'round the corner, down the hill,
Into your dungeon,—whoa, be still!
Lie down beside the sheep-skin lore,
You mischievous scamp, I'll ride no more.
A rescript comes just here from Court,
'Tis gone to the dogs, that case of tort.

THE PURE ADIPOSE.

THE ADIPOSE TISSUE;

AS EXEMPLIFIED IN THE ANDROSCOGGIN BAR.

[OCTOBER, 1877.]

[Read at a Bar Supper at DeWitt House, Feb. 7, 1882.]

I've thought of a subject that's *meat* for rhyme;
'Tis the adipose tissue, the flabby sublime;
With the good capon lined deep within and without,
Like a big bowl o' jelly it dances about,
An' shakes its broadsides of superfluous blubber
With laughter an' jest, as elastic as rubber.

The quintessence of fatness! Good nature compressed,
Bundled up in a lump, like an alderman dressed
In a suit o' fine clothes.—No skinny baboon
But a man rounded out and full orbed like the moon,
A smile from whose luminous countenance comes
Like the smile from the heart of a pudding with plums.

"Say, who do you mean, you feller of rhymes?"
Quoth chaste Brother Ludden, who swelleth sometimes;
"Why libel us fat folks for carrying around
A close corporation of bowels profound?
A spare Cassius like you plotting mischief an' war
Will encounter, by an' by, the high hand o' the law."

"Oh no, Brother Ludden, I don't mean you.
Your limbs are too shrunk, your bowels too few;
Your cheeks are too shallow, your *caput* too small,
An' your *avoirdupois* wouldn't answer at all,—
I should sooner ha' thought o' one pumpkin called *some*,
Or snapping you up once or twice on my thumb."

"Is it Record you mean, with his choker so white
That a double D.D., sir, would fit him outright?"
"Nay, I turn not on Calvin this greasy lampoon;
Too lean an' too slipper'd is his pantaloon;
His waistbands o'erlap an' too loose is his shoe,
An' his skirts hang so wide that the wind whistles thro'."

"You're thinking of Morrill, Judge Morrill, I ween,
An' he, after all, is the man that you mean;
For he is rotund and o'ershadows the ground,
An' he sees not the footsteps that trundle him 'round."
"Why, Mandeville T., so to speak of the Judge!
The thought is absurd, an' I answer you, *fudge!*

"Guess again, Brother Ludden. I'll tell ye by an' by
If ye don't guess him right." "'Tis Congressman Frye,"
Quoth chaste Brother L. "He's the biggest by far
Of all the big guns in the And'scoggin Bar."
"What a goony! Why look! Brother Frye, sir, is slim,
An' the adipose tissue hangs lightly on him.

"Give it up, d'ye say? Don't ye know there's Judge Wing,
Who's fast waxing fat like the jolly old king
O' the Cannibal Islands? He breakfasts an' sups
On none o' John Chinaman's rat soup an' pups,
But on cutlets an' sirloins, like great surrogates
Who watch o'er the widows' and orphans' estates.

"Don't ye know my friend Cotton, who tackled the bull
In the High Court arena, an' gave him a pull
By the tail? Haven't ye heard o' that wonderful feat,
An' how rough and tumble they fought the great heat?
How he had him *in law* so securely *entailed,*
How by sheer force of muscle the Bashan prevailed?

" Now, that was a deed out o' which to make fame,
And the glory thereof for friend Cotton I claim :
Do you ask what has fame with the tissue to do?
Why, it swells a man up to the bigness of two.
It distendeth his bowels, inflateth his cheek,
Till he seems with the adipose tissue to reek.

" 'Squire Hutchinson's thin and shows signs of the ravage
Of many hard fights. The implacable Savage
Looks hungry and lean : They'll never grow fat.—
You may hear their ribs rattle a rat–a–tat–tat :
No adipose there, no symptoms of gout.
You were right, Brother Ludden, in leaving them out.

" You were right, Bro. Ludden, in leaving out Moore,
Always balmy with fun tho' approaching fourscore :
But Pulsifer, Bolster, Judge Cornish and White,
Judge Dresser and Dana, pray, why did you slight?
If their claim to the adipose glory be small,
Still the oil of good nature anointeth them all.

" As for Coke on Littleton, Chitty on Bills,
Mr. Ram on Facts, and Redfield on Wills,—
They're jolly good reading to while away time,
And stir up the fancy to feats quite sublime :
The harder we study, the fatter we grow,—
But who is our Falstaff, pray, tell if you know?

" There, pass me the end of the worsted of rhyme !
You'll ne'er guess it right to the end of all time ;
I shall have to unriddle this subject of *meat*
And the adipose tissue whereof I now treat,
And say to the crowd, while the climax I cap,
That the man whom I meant all the time was Judge Knapp."

Having swung 'round the circle and compliment done
To the lights of the bar, **sir, omitting** scarce one ;
Having **curveted** high **and rhymed it full free,—**
Is any good **brother disgruntled** with me?
If he is, the best **solace I know** for his **woes**
Is a poultice spread **thick of the pure adipose.**

Oh, the adipose tissue ! I sing its renown.
Like a cushion of hair, or a pillow of down,
Or a spring-bottom bed, **it invites to repose ;**
And for surly **dyspeptics, who caw like the crows,**
'Tis the great panacea, a big, **bottled-up** laugh,—
Draw the cork and imbibe **while this bumper I** quaff !

THE STATE LIQUOR COMMISSIONER WAITED UPON.

[JULY 26, 1879.]

There is a man on Lower Main
    Whose daring deed I now relate;
A Greenback man, commissioned by
Good Gov'nor Garcelon—which is why
    He wholesales liquor for the State.

He put a sign up painted black
    Upon a board, with letters white;
The letters were three inches long.
The board was nailed up high and strong
    Behind the store, yet plain in sight.

It was no gaudy, gilded sign
    To lure the tipplers to his door;
"A simple back-door sign," said he,
" Will advertise enough for me
    My wholesale liquor dealer's store."

He did not put that sign in front,
    " Because," said he, " 'twill catch the eye
Of bold Reformers, who will crowd
Around my store and clamor loud,—
    When I don't sell it on the sly."

Vain man! To think that simple sign
    Behind the store would not be known.
Last Sunday 'twas the text whereon
They preached and speechified, till one
    Said he would lead to take it down.

" ''Twas put up to affront," he cried,
    "And to offend the public eye.
An outrage 'tis, and shall the Club
Submit, nor raise one loud hubbub?
    Why, such a Club had better die."

But moderate counsels soon prevailed :
    They chose two champions brave to wait
Upon this dealer and inform
Him of the dire, impending storm
    That soon would burst and seal his fate,

Unless he took that shocking sign
    Down from his store without delay ;
The Club meant business, and would not
Hear compromise nor yield one jot.
    Down with that sign, the leaders say.

One champion was a dentist, who
    For thirty years and something more
Had treated cases, many such,
Which other dentists would not touch,
    And probed such ulcers to the core.

The other was a lawyer, learned
    In all the law pertaining to
The case in hand, and he did look
The Maine Law thro', and then he took
    The Digest down and searched that, too.

And then decided and advised
    That 'twas illegal for the sign
To be nailed up. There was no clause
That authorized it in the Laws,
    Nor in the Digest, not a line.

So hand in hand these champions went
　　Down to this wholesale dealer's store,
And held their noses and walked in, —
Walked thro' and never barked a shin
　　Against the barrels on the floor.

And in one corner, very sly,
　　They took this dealer and made known
Their mission, and they told him how
The Club was incensed, and that now
　　The sign he promptly must take down.

No frenzy fired this dealer's eye.
　　He looked at them, and simply said :
" Be seated, friends.　All I can do
To calm the Club and comfort you
　　I'll do it, only save my head !

" My stock is choice.　Name your desire.
　　I offer freely what I have,
So far as I can legally ;
A creature of the law am I
　　And not a culprit and a knave.

" But Uncle Samuel asked of me
　　To take a license ere I sold
My stock at wholesale ; and he said
It was his custom and he made
　　His dealers all, both young and old,

" Keep up a sign to advertise
　　Their business to the public eye.
If any fail to have the sign,
Five hundred dollars is the fine
　　To pay, or else in jail they lie."

" *Ah*," quoth the dentist, " *Is that so?*
   C'est il possible, Oncle Sam? "
And here the forceps which he plied
He put away, but still he cried :
   " *Tish mighty strange indeed, py tam !* "

The lawyer next : " What, are we fools?
   Invoke for such a thing the aid
Of Uncle Sam?   As well invoke
The Bible or my great Lord Coke.
   Show me your law," he sternly said.

The dealer then took down the book,
   And read the statute, line on line,
How Uncle Samuel would impose
Fine and imprisonment on those
   Who dared to sell without a sign.

The Scriptures also he did cite :
   " ' *Woe unto* . . . *lawyers,*' which means you
Who wicked and perversely seek
A sign—with so much brazen check,
   Armed with the law and forceps, too.

" A generation evil and
   Adulterous once did seek a sign :
To them no sign at all was given
Save of the prophet Jonas, driven
   By stress of weather, not of wine,

" Into the belly of the whale,
   Where he three days and nights was kept
In durance vile, and tossed about :
Then on the dry land was spewed out,
   A sorry chap when home he crept."

The champions here did make amends.
  Apologized and kindly spoke.
They urged no more the Club's commands.
But with the dealer both shook hands,
  And said 'twas just one funny joke:

A slight misapprehension only.
  (The fumes here reached the dentist's brain.)
" *Got bless my soul, these goods are fine!*
I waives all scruples 'bout de sign;
  Oh, when shall we three meet again!""

STENOS.

THE SHORT-HAN' FELLER.

D'ye see how he does it, the short-han' feller,
  Who sits over there in the corner?
How he catches each word on his pot hook an' claps
  The story right down from those voluble chaps,
The witnesses, who, stan'in' up on their taps,
Let go the whole truth (spite the devil, perhaps,)
  Like the sage, Seth Sampson of Turner?

D'ye see how he does it, takin' it down,
  King's English an' glib Irish lingo?
Each joke an' each gesture, each laugh an' grimace
  In the turkey-track record find always a place:
He'd write the whole pack, sir, 'n the very small space
Where you couldn't write e'en the two spot or ace,—
  A wonderful feat, by jingo!

His ears are wide open, his eyes on the mark,
  He dives in his inkstand an' goes it;
No matter how fast they gabble,—what's said
  Goes down on the record, an' he keeps ahead
An' oft, when his pen at two-forty has sped,
He catches a moment an' scratches his head,
  Or kerchiefs his nose an' blows it.

Is it science or art, is it knack or device,
  Born in him or was it acquired?
'Tis a gift which yields profit no doubt very good,
  An' I think it is plain that it runs in the blood;
For he raises young short-han's (as any one would)
To transmit a vocation so well understood,
  By lawyers an' judges admired.

Since mem'ry is weak an' lawyers dispute,
　　An' indulge oftentimes in dissensions;
Saying, "Witness said so, as my minutes show,"
　　An', "Witness said *contra* I'd have ye to know;"
Since judges forget they have charged so an' so,
How sweet to the short-han' reporter to go
　　An' settle all hash o' contentions.

An' then when the jurors get sleepy an' dull,
　　Hearin' all the whole truth till they're snory,
An' their minds wander off to affairs o' their own,
　　An' the issue drops out o' their thoughts like a stone,—
How 'n thunder could they, when so jaded they've grown,
Tell which o' the dogs had the right to the bone,
　　Or remember the witnesses' story?

But the short-han' feller, he never takes naps;
　　He's on the *qui vive* when the jury
Wilt down after dinner, and nod in their seats,
　　Like deacons at church in the dog-day heats.
If the lawyer fires up, or the witness repeats,
No storm o' confusion his record defeats;
　　He writes the whole fracas like fury.

O marvelous man! A great wonder you be!
　　You spells it an' makes it good grammar,
An' you gets it all in. Not a cough or a sneeze
　　That belongs to the case but you note it with ease.
Do you dot all your i's, sir, and cross all your t's
When you drive at two-forty, or thirty, 'f you please,
　　In the midst of a hubbub an' clamor?

Say, what will you take for to teach us your art,
　　We chaps that sit inside the bar,
An' also the judges, who need some relief,

The associates, indeed, as well as the chief?
Can't we have the opinions as well as each brief
Hereafter writ out in good pot-hook relief,
    Perspicuous an' clear as a star?

Say, what would you take for to do it up brown
    An' elucidate all that's obscure,—
Comin' right to the point like a fish to the hook,
    Makin' argument run just as clear as a brook,
Then nailin' the thing, with a logical look,
More firm than 'tis nailed in the sheep-skin book?
    The meshes, I guess, would be fewer.

We'd have the great principles settled an' fixed,
    Beyond peradventure of *quære!*
The light of the bench, an' the bar should shine forth
    In a blaze stenographic,—an era have birth
When our fees should be up to our services' worth,
An' the horn of our *Stenos* exalted on earth,—
    " *Monumentum perennius ære.*"

TRU FILLOSSOFY OV KORRECK SPELLIN,

AS LADE DOWN BY STENOS.

[JUNE 12, 1875.]

[Many will remember the mania for spelling that overran the country a few years ago. The interest in Auburn was so great that public meetings were held at Auburn Hall, and persons who were proficient in the art entered the lists and made public exhibition of their skill in spelling. It was reported at the time that our good friend, "Stenos," was one of the champions, and that by some unaccountable slip of the tongue he failed on the common word, "*firkin*." The fault, however, I believe, was attributable in part to the fellow who put out the words. *Hinc illae lachrymae!*]

Sez J. D. P., in spellin, sez he,
    The fust rool to be follered is this :
Fust, pik out a pheller ov bottom and brane
To put out the wurds. Kommand him speke plane ;
Ef he klips the sillerbuls, rapp with yer kane
An' make him enunshate over agane ;
An' then from his phault ef he don't refrane,
Jus pile him away with the victims he's slane,
    Purnouncin the wurds amys.

Sez J. D. P., I tel 'e, sez he,
    Thers 2 ways this biznes to du,—
Sum spels by the site, an some by the sounde :
The eer's the bes gide my experens has founde ;
Butt wen a grate speller is lade on the grounde,
An phlounders an kicks an dyes with his wounde,
Tiz generly bekaws the purnouncin's unsounde,
Not accordin to Webbstur an uthers perfounde,
    But vulghar, deseteful, untru.

The seckkond grate rool, sez J. D. P.,
    Wen yuve gut the purnouncin set rite,
Is, pictur the wurd speld out in yer ey ;
Purnounce it yerself be 4 spellin yu tri.
Doant spit on yer hans like a jimnast an kri,
Yu challenge the wurld in this kontest tu vy ;
Butt konsentrate the forse ov yer eere an yer ey,
Then karmly yer volley ov letturs let fli,—
    I tel 'e, yu'll spel like a kite.

Beware ov the pheller, sez J. D. P.,
    Who poots the wurd "*furkin*" out thus,—
Who aksents the *furk* an jumps over the *in*,
Then looks in yer fase with an innersent grinn,
An asks yu to spel. He's for takin yu in.
H's a heethen Chinee, ful as bad as Ar Sinn.
He'll trap yu 'f he kan on the sillerbul " *in*,"
Then larf at yer flummucks, yer shame an shagrinn.
    I despize such a mizabul kus.

Tiz no sine of a duns, sez J. D. P.,
    Ef the speller shud spel it *e-n*.
No sine he is bilyous, or week in the bak,
Or unsounde in the brane ; no sine ov a krak
In his kranium, wich holds, as it wer, in a sak
His hole budgit ov lore ; no sine ov a lak
Ov resurch in the grate *Unabridged*, in hoos trak
He's follered for yeres, an lernt the grate knak
    How to spel with his tung an his penn.

The truth is kwite obvius, sez J. D. P.,
    That a expurt, who deels in short han
An spels wurds by sines kabballistic all thru,
Very much as they spels in the land of Lu Chu,
Kant ollers kepe sistems distinct in his view.

He's gut on his side the grate axium, tu,
That sum wurds is speld rite in won way an 2,—
What a ass is the koxkom who ses tiz untru !
    Wun *furkin* would hold such a man.

I apele to Jedge Napp, sez J. D. P.,
    Hoose genyus for **spellin is grate,**
Original, an hily **inventiv,—nay more,**
Jedge Napp never **yit, sir,** was lade on the flore.
He spels wurds in **wun way,** or **2, three** an **fore,**
Espeshaly the **klassic wurd,** *pig-pen phlowre.*
Wen the Hi Jedge asked, **was it** pozy or phlore,
Jedge Napp set the **cort room** all in a rore,
    Speken up, with his har stanin **strate :**

'' Pleze yer **Onner, I say the man is a phool,**
    Who kant spel more **waize 'an wun.**
Thers no such a **lunk in th' Andskoggin Baa,**
From Kotton, Wing, and Hutch down to Hossly's little star ;
Wun so feerful dull as that, is tu muddlehead **by far**
Tu pracktis as atturny in a Hi Cort ov Lor."
So the **Hi** Judge larft with a *haw, haw, haw,*
An didn't fine Napp for his orthograflic phlaw
    In his pig-pen flore.   **I've dun.**

COOK'S DIVIDEND.

[Lines congratulatory to J. G. Cook, Dec. 5, 1877, on his receiving a dividend of four cents from the estate of G. S. Plummer, bankrupt.]

Dear Cook :   The dawn of better days
    Is breaking o'er this famished land :
Plummer's estate a tribute pays
    At sight, or promptly on demand.

Your claim of sixteen sixty-seven,
    Proved 'gainst the assets and allowed,
Draws just four cents.   Give thanks to Heaven,
    O lucky man ! but don't be proud.

Almost a nickel !   Hold your mirth,
    And persevere, for foresight wins :
A woman once confined, brought forth
    And lack'd but one of having twins.

But here the fee comes back to you,
    A dollar and four cents besides :
Keep up your courage, don't get blue,
    Kind Providence o'er all presides.

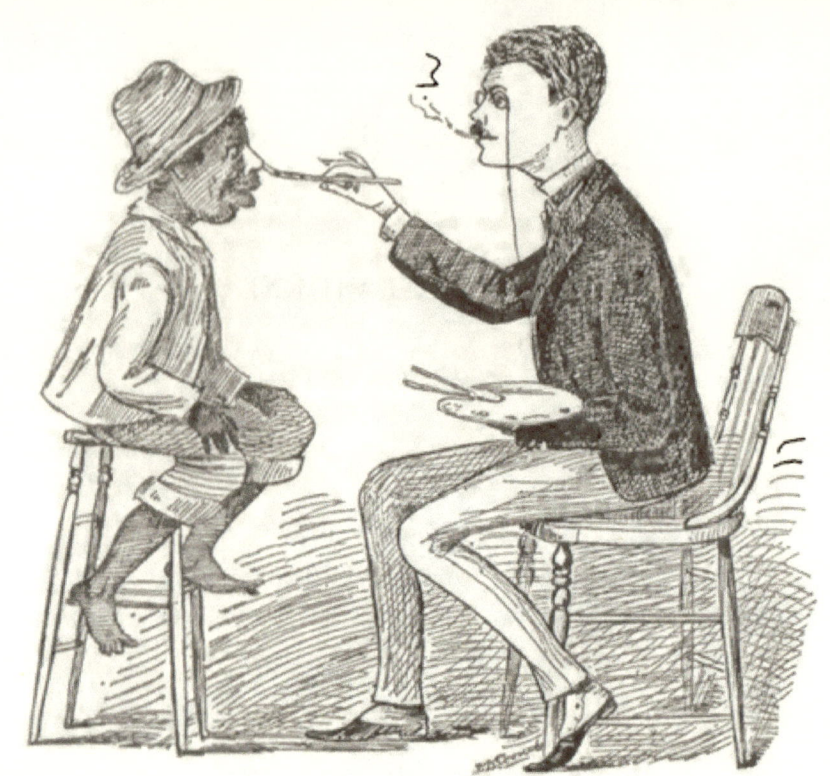

A FREAK OF ART.

THE IMP OF FAME.

I read an•item in the paper,
A brief account of one queer caper,
Cut up somewhere in Ohio,
Within an artist's studio;
A freak for fun, which by mishap
Turned out to have an afterclap.

The artist was a fancy man,
No one-horse artist, but a span.
He drove a black one and a red,
Matched up for contrast, as he said;
And with his rare, artistic eye
He wrought strange contrasts on the sly.

One day into his studio
'Way out somewhere in Ohio,
A cullud youth with woolly head,
Flat nose, thick lips lined ruby red,
Came saying, " Ise an errand boy,
And wants to git me some employ."

" No errands," said the artist man;
" I only keeps one black and tan.
But, Sambo, try your luck in paint:
I've thought of something rich and quaint.
Five cents for you I here propose
If you will let me paint your nose,

" And just one errand for me then
Do promptly, like a little man."
" Yis, Massa." Sambo laughed to think
How easy he should earn the chink ;
And soon beneath the magic brush
His little nose began to blush,

Changing its hue from dark to red
As free the pigment on was spread.
" There, Bully Boy ! Don't sneeze or snuff ;
Don't touch that nose, nor rub it off ;
But up the street to number nine
Stiver along (you'll see the sign),

" Call on the man there, artist Hood,
Tell him a youth of royal blood,
An imp of fame, before him stands,
Ready to do his high commands.
Tell him the pedigree he shows
Is cullud like his royal nose."

Off started Sambo, prompt, intent,
On errand and on money bent ;
Conning his message o'er and o'er,
Tho' "pedigree" oft stuck him sore ;
Doing his level best to say
It straight, and so secure the pay.

Ah, many topers on the street,
With noses red, did Sambo meet,
And many urchins hooting loud,
That jeered him passing thro' the crowd ;
And soon a rabble they became,
Hard pressing the poor imp of fame.

They seized and caught him, just as he
Stuck on the great word "*pedigree*."
" No darkey boy," those urchins swore,
" Was e'er got up like him before :
We must take off that gay, red nose,
Red lips is all the law allows."

They took him to a boot-black then,
To have his nose shined black again,—
One of those expert boot-black fellers,
Who said he'd shine the darkey's smellers
For just three cents (a half-price rate),
And bring 'em to their normal state.

Just here a cullud woman came
And looked upon the imp of fame,
And when she saw his visage mild
She screamed aloud : " *My bressed child !*
Put down that boy, you brats," said she,
" *Lor' bress yer, honey,* come *wid me*."

She took him home and soaped his face,
And rubbed his nose till not a trace
Of royal blood or pedigree
Was left for any eye to see.
The artist's skill was all in vain,
Lo, Sambo was himself again.

But when he told his dismal tale,
It made the cullud folks turn pale,
And vengeance on the artist swear.
They posted to a lawyer there,
Friend of the down-trod cullud race,
And laid before him all the case.

He up and sued the artist man,
Him of the two-horse dashing span,
And laid the damage high and strong,
And put it to the jury long,
And spoke of civil rights, declaring
That for a deed so red and glaring,

Vindictive damage should be found
The artist should be punished sound;
Compelled to paint his own nose black
Or suffer torture on the rack.
These weighty words the jury pondered
Till half the panel were dumfoundered.

They soon retired, discussed, and laid
Their heads together, and they said:
"Sure, this facetious artist man
For his rare fun must stan' his han';
No darkey boy, whate'er his name,
Shall thus be made an imp of fame.

"Let dancers pay the fiddler's fee,
No matter what the pedigree."
So, on a verdict they agreed
(Let every artist man take heed):
"*Guilty,*" the foreman made report.
"*Fine, one round hundred,*" said the Court.

PHIL SHERIDAN.

THE YELLOW DOG THAT FOLLOWS ME.

Some dogs march boldly thro' the street,
Contemptuous of all men they meet.
You whistle them, and say: "Good pup!"
They snarl enough to eat you up;
And prowling go like beasts of prey,
While cautious folks keep out the way.
Such fiendish curs deserve cold lead
Imbedded promptly in the head.

Some other dogs play scaly cards
As trespassers in folks' back yards,
Nosing swill pails with no misgivin'.
Stealing, in fact, full half their livin'.
You say to one: "You scamp, get out!"
The pilferer you may put to rout;
But look for him again next day,
No booting keeps such scamps away.

But better-natured dogs there are,
Of better principles by far,—
Dogs that don't bite and seldom steal.
And real fondness for you feel.
Some carry little curled-up tails,
Whose wag of friendship never fails:
And best of all this class is he,
The yellow dog that follows me.

He's fat and sleek ; and he can eat
More dinner than I dare repeat,
And sometimes I have honest fear
Dyspepsia may o'ertake him here.
To tell his faults is not my whim,
I'm not the man to tell on him ;
So fast a friend of mine is he,
The yellow dog that follows me.

He playeth many pretty pranks,
Sits up like Major on his shanks,
As straight as monkeys or baboons.
I know his natural pantaloons
Are worn behind almost threadbare :
They'll soon be thro'—his only pair—
And winter coming fierce will see
A shivering dog, I fear, with me.

Phil Sheridan is his good name ;
That smacks a dashing warrior's fame,
But *Phil* hath a distaste for war,
And when there's fighting lurks afar :
In peaceful parlors loves to dwell,—
Sometimes when callers ring the bell
He breaks the peace and is uncivil,
And barketh like a little devil.

Timid of war, he's fond of fun :
Will give all cats that start and run
A vigorous chase, till they show fight,
Then he retreats with all his might ;
Remembering always from the start,
Prudence is valor's better part.
Ah, once or twice he hath had cause
To dread an old cat's teeth and claws.

He sits beside me when I dine,
And watches all my bread and wine:
You'd laugh to see the rogue implore
And ask, like Oliver, for more.
And when I take my hat to leave,
He's ready, you may well believe:
They never fool'd him yet but he
Somehow gets out and follows me.

I stick by him, he sticks by me;
Yet ofttimes when the pesky flea
Is prowling thro' his yellow hair,
And worries him so sorely there,—
" Phil, catch your fleas! This is to pay
For going with low-bred dogs," I say.
" Keep better company, and be
Free from your foe,—the pesky flea."

THE CHEVALIER.

IO TRIUMPHE!!

A NEW-YEAR'S RHYME FOR 1874.

I am the feller, I whisper to you,
Who crowed for the city in 'seventy-two,—
The self-same feller, who New-Year's Day
Saddled his steed and passed this way,
In the early light of the glimmering morn,
To herald the birth of the year new born.

Over the bridge, ere the whistle of steam
Had startled the town with its matin scream,
Or the heavy stroke of the larum bell
Had broken the charm of the dreamer's spell,
I passed on that strange, fantastical raid,
In the hoar-frost drapery white arrayed,—
With visor and helm and dancing plume,
Careering along thro' the morning gloom
Like a phantom knight, who sallies forth
From the crystal halls of the frozen north,
With mail and trappings reflecting bright
The hues of the first auroral light.

I cared not a fig for the barking curs
That followed behind, but, plying the spurs,
I pranced along through the city streets,
Tho' alleys and by-ways and sly retreats,
Past the temple where the button chaps keep,
And down by the blocks where the mill girls sleep;
Doubling the corners and riding so brisk.
I was gone ere one could ejaculate, *whisk!*

I then struck out o'er gully and hill,
Out where the suburbs are somber and still,
To the outermost skirt of the spindle town,
Where the city stops at a stake drove down.

D'ye say I spin this rhyme to deceive,
And tell such a whopper none can believe,—
That the woof and the warp of the whole discourse
Are false, and assert I can't ride a horse?
Pray who are you, you lubber, you lout,
To bring such a narrative thus into doubt,
To spoil such a story running so fine,
Setting my verses awry, out of line?
I'll wager my beard, a bottle beside,
You snoozed in your bed while I did ride,
You snored like a pig, with a guttural snore,—
Get out o' my way, and bodder no more.

Again I am here in 'seventy-four,
On the same proud steed I rode before,
Accoutered the same, and I ply the spurs,
And care not a fig for the barking curs.
I caper all nimbly, and wave salute
As gracious as General Grant can do't.
(Here's a little hiatus, as you will see,
I've missed, in my haste, year 'seventy-three.
There's reason for this quite valid, no doubt,
I then got married and couldn't get out.)

You may think, indeed, 'tis shivering sport
For a chap like me, of the sober sort,
To be capering thus, and deem, perhaps,
I'd better be down upon my taps,
Slapping my hands with lusty slaps,

Rapping my feet with vigorous raps,
To keep out the teeth o' the biting cold
That takes of an in-door man such hold.
I've something inside that keeps me warm :
Elixir of life—don't raise an alarm—
I take it straight, this magical balm,
It keeps the cold out o' me like a charm.

'Tis two long years since, frisky and spry,
I paraded the town (how time goes by !)
On New-Year's morn, proclaiming good cheer,
Prosperity, peace, and a happy New Year.
I've not grown old, nor rheumaticky much,
Like the twain who skate, drink cider, and such ;
Tho' the frosts of years have sprinkled somewhat
This beard, once glossy and brown as a nut.
Thank Heaven for pluck ! I seldom do brag,
But I think just now with my mettlesome nag
I could challenge the world, and even go by
The skating old lady, so spunky and spry,
With smut on her nose and cider within,
Tho' skating a flagon of cider to win.

In twenty-four months behold how the pride
Of the town has advanced ! The codger outside,
Who comes along from the neighboring town,
Beyond the place where the stake's drove down,
Much marvels to see the marshals and mayors,
The aldermen, councilmen, city purveyors,
The great brick temple with steeple so high
(Not so high as the cost, I remark, by the by),
The grand bazar, the plaza, DeWitt,
The mansions where nabobs and mill agents sit,

5

The rôle of the fashions, the livery, the style,
Whose glories no panic on earth can despoil.
Ah, countrymen meek, in the market to-day,
Standing round for a bid for your wood and **your hay,**
Gazing long **at** the moneyed folks, passing so quick,—
Sell only for cash, and never on tick.
There are snobs, I've heard, in this city of mills,
Who, **fast at all else, are slow** paying bills.
They take advantage of clever folks, too,
In a measly way, I whisper to you,—
A bad state of things, unjust and unlawful,—
I know of a countryman says it is awful.

But I spread too much ; I must here draw in,
And let not the tissue of **rhyme grow thin :**
Milk and water for babies will very well **do,**
But never for full-grown **folks, I trow.**

I'm proud **of** this **city—Ili-yah, Hi-yah !**
Proud as John Bull **was over the Shah,**
Proud as New Yorkers were over Jim **Fisk,**
Proud of the fabrics whose tissues we **twist ;**
Proud of **our** pluck, **sir, proud of the way**
We've kept the panic financial at bay,
Proud o' the great men, especially proud
Of the ladies whose praises **I** warble aloud ;
Proud o' the milliners,—what should we **do**
If they should *bust up* when panics ensue?
Proud o' the sleighriders,—fellers and gals,
Dashing along past the **gingerbread** stalls,
Billing and cooing along the **highway**
Like turtle-doves wooing **in April or May ;**
Proud o' the **enterprise, bustle and** stir,
Proud **o' the gloss o' the velvet** and fur,
Proud **as** the deacons **of** Pine Street are,
Proud as a little boy is **of his** pa.

D'ye wonder how 'tis I hold so much pride
And still on my Pegasus manage to ride,
How 'tis I confine such volatile stuff,
And never explode and go off in a puff?
I'll tell ye 'bout that on some other time,
Just here 'twould impede the grand march o' my rhyme.
Which now is quite up to the monkey sublime.

Enough, enough! I here draw off,
But never my visor and helm shall doff.
Enough! The circuit is now complete:
The bantam hath crowed, and I retreat.
I vanish, I'm gone; I pass from view
Like a mist which the morning light goes through.
No more for a twelvemonth, now, I presume
Will you catch the gleam of my dancing plume,
Or see the horseman, encased in mail,
Astride o' the nag with flowing tail,
Prancing the streets at early dawn,
To herald the birth of a year new-born.

THE JULEPS.

Mint and anise, rye and cumin,
These I put in when I mix 'em;
And I stir 'em with a teaspoon
    Till you hardly smell the rye.
But there's science in the mixin',
And the rule is, so to make 'em
That a deacon, staid and sober,
    May imbibe and not get high.

Want me to disclose this secret?
By what art I do compound 'em,
How I make 'em so majestic,
    With the rhymes all flowing free?
Whence I draw my inspiration,
Why the deuce I don't slop over
When I put on such a pressure,
    And you wonder so at me?

Ah, you fellers, I'll not answer
How this business is conducted.
You may say: "His Muse is boosy,
    Or she ne'er would cut up so."
I shall hang on to my secret.
If you thorn me, I shall speak up
Pretty short, and say: "Confound you!
    It's a thing you'll never know."

THE JULEPS.

Better far you hark and listen,
Better give your whole attention
To the process of this grinding:
    I take hold and turn the **crank**,
This machine gives out the music.
It **will** tune up loud and louder,
And the monkey will be playful
    Or **his chain'll get a** yank.

Don't be fussy, **don't be** squamish,
Please more softly blow your **noses;**
Have you got the epizootic?
    Is it on you all to-night?
Try a little gentle **ginger**,
Some specific which the doctors
Recommend for *idfluedza*,—
    In a moment **you'll** be right.

Now I give you the refreshments,
Give you cakes right from the griddle,
Give you taffy with the sardines,
    Which you haven't had before.
Now fall **to and have** your spero.
Lo, this poem marcheth on**ward!**
I shall stir the fragrant **juleps**
    Till you cease **to cry,** *encore*.

Hark, **the steam is up.** She **buzzes:**
Now she **booms! But what's that crackin'?**
What the dickens ails my elbow?
    Ah, **I feel so mighty queer:**
Let me **blow a little vapor**,
Let me ease somewhat the **pressure**,
Lest there be a dire **explosion**,
    Lest these juleps burst me here.

Goodness, gracious! Who'd a thought it?
Who'd a thought to see the poet
All fush out like a sky-rocket,
    Flinging far his trump of fame?
Oh, good brothers, do not name it.
'Tis with shame I do confess it :
Too much rye was in the mixin',
    'Twas the juleps were to blame.

'Tis not often thus I miss it,
But sometimes the mint and anise
And the aromatic cumin
    Bother me to fix 'em right :
Ere I think I lose discretion
When I use the rye and teaspoon,
And I make a wide departure
    Which a deacon would affright.

THE POETICAL MAN.

I see him on the streets sometimes,
A man forlorn, who lacketh dimes :
With seedy coat and last year's hat,
And cheeks collapsed for want of fat.

His nose is sharp, his ears are thin,
A sickly hue is on his skin ;
His uncut nails are darkly draped,
No knife, no soap, he goes unscraped.

Seldom he mixes with the crowd ;
His words are few and never loud,
His faults not many,—only drinks
To cut the cobwebs when he thinks.

Now, by the learn'd professions three,
What specimen of man is he,
Who, owl-like, thinks when on the streets,
And speaks no living soul he meets ;

But wanders on as if possessed
Of something hard to be expressed,
And oftimes 'neath the sultry sky
" In a fine frenzy" rolls his eye?

Why doth he toil and sweat all day
In such unprofitable way,
And then at night up garret sleep
Where prowling bugs victorious creep?

Why in his dreams do owls and imps
And wrinkled hags with horrid crimps,
And devils blue, and devils green,
Dance nightmare in a ghostly scene?

O fascination of the Muse !
What mortal man, without the blues,
Could live such life, and waste his time
In blowing bubbles into rhyme !

So many a vain, presumptuous wight,
Who's sought to scale Parnassus' height,
Has turned to nought his hopes and wares,—
Bad luck, for which nobody cares !

Law, gospel, medicine may give
Enough, perchance, for one to live ;
But slipshod dreaming all the day,
As a profession, does not pay.

For nought times nought **just nothing gives** :
An axiom which no fool that lives
Can e'er disprove by writing reams
Upon the moonshine's watery beams.

'Tis pleasant to inscribe a name
Illustrious on the rolls of fame ;
'Tis nice **to have a coat** that's new,
A shiny hat, a meerschaum, too ;

And sweet to loll in easy chair
And say, avaunt, to cankering care ;
But, O my friend, depressed and **blue,**
These joys are not in store **for you.**

No habitation, **not a name,**
Not one poor flash of fickle fame,
Not e'en a perch whereon to cling
And rest at last a weary wing,—

Such are the ill-starred fates of those
Who, not content with sober prose,
Venture that treach'rous sea t' **explore**
Where bards are shipwreck'd by the score.

Pity the poor, poetic man !
Persuade him, if indeed you can,
To cease his wanderings 'round the **town,**
Cease his eternal study, brown.

Lend him your knife and cake of soap ;
Inspire him **with a better hope** ;
Advise him not to **sleep so high,**
So far from earth, so near the sky.

Give him a dime, in his sore need,
Wherewith to bate his jaded steed.
Only a dime!   And mark how true
His harp will ring response to you!

Only a dime!   The organ man,
Who turns a penny where'er he can,
Would charge no more for one long grind,
With show of the monkey an' tail behind.

Only a dime!   Enough, adieu!
Enough! His heart will throb for you,
And then the lyre's resistless sway
Will drive the shadows grim away.

EPISTLE TO H. GREELEY.

[Addressed to him at the time of his presidential aspirations, in 1872, by the young man whom he advised to go West.]

My ancient friend! I am perplexed:
My politics is half unsexed;
Pray, what will you be up to next
      With your old hob?
You lead a rabble, strangely mixed,
      Rag, tag, and bob.

What puzzles me the most is this,—
To see *those same*, that used to hiss
And sneer at you, now come and kiss
      Your garment skirts,
And shower you o'er with words o' bliss,
      And loving spurts.

Are you with them, or they with you?
Pray, tell us which,—we want to know.
It kind o' seems to me, somehow,
      You're off the track,
And coat and hat, to avoid a row,
      You'd best turn back.

But, Horace, you're a set old feller ;
'F I counseled you till all was yeller,
Yea, *Tribune* like, if I should beller
      What I thought best ;
You'd say : " Young man, your brain is meller,
      There's farms out West."

Oh, onest you were a gallant Whig !
You made the Locos reel and jig
In the old days o' the " Striped Pig,"
      Hard cider times ;
And now you offer them a swig,
      With all their crimes.

Free Soil was once your hobby horse ;
Then " Bleeding Kansas," shaped your course,
You charged on ruffian frauds and force,
      Coat tail a flyin' ;
And when Rebellion's hordes broke loose,
      Fought 'em to dyin'.

Ah, what a dose for them you be !
How from such physic they would flee
If other nostrum they could see
      A sight to follow !
They'll all be sick, I'll bet a V,
      When you they swallow.

For amnesty you go it strong ;
No matter what the crime and wrong,
" One happy family," is now your song ;
      " Couvulsion o'er,
We'll sleep together, loving long,
      And sin no more."

Well, go it, Horace!   You know best
What side to take in this contest;
You are a sage with foresight blest
   To see what's comin';
Don't squat the eagle on a nest
   That's foul with vermin.

Say, if elected, shall you take
Jeff Davis into your grand wake,
And give him chance the dice to shake
   O'er loaves and fishes?
His bondsmen should, for friendship's sake,
   Consult his wishes.

Oh, Horace, Horace!   When you tell
Of farming which you know so well,
And show us how we may excel
   In that vocation;
Explain, I pray you, if you will,
   U. S. plantation.

Explain how 'tis, on that grand scale,
The art of farming can prevail;
So we may try the scythe and flail
   'Gainst opposition,
And cut and thresh all who assail
   Our high ambition.

Consider, sir!   You must not win
With such support to help you in;
Nay, sooner, we will all begin
   Doin' extra courtin',
And try to save you from this sin
   By women's votin'.

We stand by Grant, **who stood by us**
Thro' **all** the foul, rebellious muss,
An' never said to them, " Poor Puss,"
       But drove 'em howlin' ;
Why now desert 'n a trumped-up fuss
       Wi' those chaps prowling?

Excuse **me, sir,** this little **note**
Will make **no** difference **in the vote** ;
I still respect **your hat and coat,**
       Tho' they need dusting ;
The changes, sir, since last I wrote
       Are quite disgusting.

COMPLIMENTS OF THE SEASON.

If a sensible man may whistle and sing
  In this land of the frozen North,
What marvel that I should do such a thing
As yield to the voice of the laughing spring,
  And let these words go forth?

Somehow, a breath of the genial air,
  And a glance of the warm sunshine,
Will start my warble ere I am aware;
And I spin out a rhyme quite debonair,
  To humor this whim of mine.

But the laughing spring did I say, and still
  Do I prate of that blissful time?
What bosh! I stand here and shake with the chill,
And a blast sweeps down from the northern hill,
  Killing the soul of my rhyme.

Oh! the poets may tune us a vernal strain,
  Of sunshine, blossom, and flowers,
With never a hint, to the last refrain,
Of the pestilent slosh, the mud, and the rain,
  That rule this spring-time of ours.

But who will chant on the long delay
  Of the April showers till June?
Who'll harp on the storm that howls all day,
Or the dreary drizzle that quencheth the ray
  Of the genial sun at noon?

If a wandering gleam of the sunshine warms
    And prompteth your heart to sing,
Go forth and enjoy the season's charms,
And,—slump in a snow-drift up to your arms,
    In the midst of "the beautiful spring."

I tell you the romance all fades before
    You walk the length of the street;
The March wind comes with a sinister roar,
Your hat goes down to the furthest store,
    While you go off from your feet.

Ay, worse than this does the laughing spring:
    It inveigles the ladies abroad,
And then, with its gusts on the mischievous wing,
Plays deuce with the skirts and the mantles,—a thing
    I verily blush to record.

O spirit of Thompson, enshrined with the bards!
    Enough of your "dropping cloud"!
We stick by our firesides playing at cards,
No "shadowing roses" adorn our door-yards,
    But a snow-bank is there like a shroud.

Excuse me, my friend of poetical turn,
    For exposing the prose of the thing;
If you will strike the lyre in a season so stern,
Just encourage the hope of the summer's return,
    Dry up on "the beautiful spring."

MRS. McFUDDLE.

ELIZA JANE PROTESTS.

Who tole that lie, so sthrappan an' big,
    Was printed last night in the paper,
'Bout me overhauled by perlice in the cars
Wi' a two-gallon jug, a defyin' the laws?
    My soul! what a villainous caper.

Arrah, I jist knows the feller that tole
    That dastardly lie, an' I cares not
For his buttons an' badge an' pretintions at all;
'Twas Towle was the man that tole it—that's all,
    Spalpeen, deny it he dares not.

6

An' I knows jist as well who tole all the rest,
  'Bout the sore on my nose (that's got well now) ;
Does he think I've no pride o' my person to-day?
Who's the meanest? To trate a poor woman that way,—
  Divil shake such a brute till he yell, now.

An' then all that stuff 'bout me an' my trade,
  Calling me " the old ancient retailer,"
Meaning I was a dealer in contraband drinks,
Which is lie to the bottom,—a scandal that stinks ;
  What trash in the world could be staler?

Let him write his name " Ed." an' so try to deceive,
  But I knows him, as well as that Towle :
He peddles out papers,—to him I replies :
He's an " ancient retailer" himself of old lies
  About me, an' 'tis many he's tole.

'Tween drinks an' such stories, now, where is the odds?
  By the glass or the paper dealt out?
Sold at ten cents or three, by myself or that " Ed.,"
Which " ancient retailer," I ask, is ahead,
  An' which should be first put to rout?

I protests against Towle an' the stories he tole ;
  He did not seize liquor from me ;
An' the feller that writes his name " Ed.," to disguise,
I protests against all his fantastical lies :
  Sure, Mrs. McFuddle speaks free.

An' she steps to the front,—Marshal Douglass give
      heed !
  Look out for that Towle with the women ;
'Tis no jug he is after, hid under the dress,
No breach of the laws that he seeks to repress ;
  His brain in a fever is swimmin'.

But I keeps to myself a good part that I knows,
    Might damage the case o' that Towle,—
Takin' jugs from poor women, out under their clothes,
In the cars where folks travels,—bad conduct, which
       shows
Him indacint an' rude, 'pon my soul!

So I keeps to myself a good part that I knows,—
    But I knows that my nose is all right;
An' I doesn't sell drinks, an' I doesn't tell lies,
An' I minds my business, an' will till I dies;
    But Towle keep out o' my sight!

TO THE CULLER OF STAVES.

[At the city election in Lewiston, 1879, our genial friend, Charles W. Waldron, Esq., of the *Gazette*, was triumphantly re-elected to the office of Culler of Staves.]

Charlie again has turned a trump,—
 Charlie, in whom myself belaves.
Speed, Pegassus, now flap an' jump,
I give my lyre an **extra** thump
 For such a boy to cull the staves.

He's faithful been, both day an' night,
 Fidelity **his bacon saves** ;
Now twelve months more, the hoops all right,
We know the barrels will be **tight,**
 For Charlie, he will cull the staves.

I care not how perverse may be
 The politics 'bout which one raves ;
The one important thing with **me**
Is just to have a man who'll be
 Above a bribe **in** cullin' **staves.**

All other cullers, since the **war,**
 Have sunk beneath **oblivion's waves** ;
But Charlie's bright, ascendant star
Shines like **a torch of** burnin' tar,—
 Such glory comes o' cullin' staves.

Now genial Spring comes on apace,
　An' surly March no longer raves ;
Soon will the school-girls romp an' chase,
An' hunt the May-flower's hiding place,—
　Look out, young culler of the staves !

Can you resist Dan Cupid's powers ?
　Suppose some game that urchin craves,
An' opes to you his rosy bowers,
Where all the girls are cullin' flowers,—
　Would you not falter cullin' staves ?

The best advice I have to spare
　Is, shun Dan Cupid, prince o' knaves ;
He'll trap ye sudden, unaware,
An' shoot ye thro' the heart, somewhere,—
　Who then would cull the hoops an' staves ?

We'll let ye sometimes share the bliss
　A culler should, who well behaves :
Ye may go sparkin' with a Miss,—
Whose business if ye cull a kiss
　To cheer ye weary cullin' staves ?

The barrels always will be tight
　(The culler never, I belaves).
Cull on, my boy, an' cull 'em right ;
Fling all the bad ones out o' sight,
　Pass only merchantable staves.

THE CITY MISSIONARY.

The city missionary's name
　　Is simply Plum,
Or sometimes Plummer, oftener Plum.
　　He's not from Rome,
Nor unction from the church doth claim;
But here he hath been known to fame
For years, a long, well-rounded score.
　　Not Father Plum,
　　Not Reverend Doctor Plum,
But simply Plum and nothing more.

His sanctum, documents, and keys
　　He keeps up there,
Snug in the great, brick chapel, where
　　The jail birds share,
Daily with him his bread and cheese;
But chiefly he subsists on fees.
He makes long circuits thro' the town,
　　And country, too,
　　Finds heaps o' work to do,
And fearless gathers in his own.

No special air of sanctity
　　Doth he assume;
He dons no robe of priestly gloom,
　　Just for a boom;
Thinks not o'er much of titles, he
Ne'er cared a d— for a D.D.
His work is for the public weal:
　　He lays his hand,
　　Sometimes with stern command,
On ruffians who break thro' and steal.

Conspicuous man is he in court,
    Keeps order there,
Pounds on his desk enough to scare
    All who should dare
Disturb the bench of last resort.
Woe to the scamp who should retort
On him, grand mogul, armed with power!
    His business 'tis
    The noisy crowd to quiz
Till at his spectral nod they cower.

His flock he gathers in his fold,
    And he doth call
Them often to confessional,
    And, one and all,
Protects from pitfalls manifold.
And he hath virtues, too, untold,
And impulses, humane and jolly,
    Which grace him there,—
    Tho' he sometimes will flare
And utter uncouth words a volley.

We ne'er will let him leave his post
    For heathen lands,
Where cannibals, in hungry bands,
    With bloody hands,
The missionary kill and roast,
And eat him up,—all save his ghost.
Perish the heathen ere he go!
    Such martyrdom
    For generous, faithful Plum
Shall never be. No, never, no!

MY GRAND EPIC.

As one who muses when the whistle blows,
And feels misgivings tingling to his toes,
And hears the bells and counts the numbers o'er,
But cannot leave, tho' fire is at his door;
Who still keeps musing with strange unconcern,
Nor ceases ever while the fire doth burn;
So I have mused and searched the stars in vain
For something, brothers, meet to entertain;
Some rhyme in prose, or prose in rhyme to bring,
A medley one may whistle, or may sing.

Perhaps some story or some legend queer,
Would suit your tastes and win for me a cheer;
Or, if you're bilious and have shakes and chills,
Perhaps a few compound, cathartic pills,
Done up in rhyme, would stir you up to-night,
Clear off the bile, and set your spirits right.
What e'er it be, dull, lively, or abstruse,
Or marvelous strains, like those of Mother Goose,
I pray you listen,—give attentive ear,
For 'twill be long ere you the like will hear.
You will perceive I'm not a deaf-and-dumb bug,
But quite a star, and surely not a humbug.

The poet wrestles till his lyre's in tune,
Then up he rises, much like a balloon;
To mortal man it is a thing unknown
How, when, and where the poet will come down.
Bard of to-day soars high upon the wing,
And never harps upon a single string;

And he hath many queer, fantastic ways,
Which beat the world and shame the ancient lays.
He doth not bore with one heroic strain,
As Homer did when Troy was on his brain.
He hath not got King David's tone and phiz;
Not Milton's song, nor Shakespeare's line is his.
They are not models for this modern bard,
Who always plays his own, peculiar card.
But 'tis important I should start all right,
And reel off stanzas in good style to-night.
'Tis always true, in rhyming as in spinning,
The place to start is right at the beginning.

Far back, before the days of prose and rhyme,
About coeval with the birth of time,
Events began, and some there were took place
Of vast importance to the human race.
First, the creation,—when from chaos wild
The earth was formed, and in the sunlight smiled.
This was a big improvement on the old,
Chaotic state of things 'bout which we're told.
It gave foundation and, in fact, a place,—
Some foot-hold for the coming human race.
It opened fields for agriculture, trade,—
Things which in chaos never would have paid.
It cleared the way for fine arts, which, 'twould seem,
Could not have flourished in the old *régime*.

Next Adam's make, first living man that stirred:
He was a social fellow, and preferred
Gay company. He e'en gave up his bone,
Rather than eat his garden sauce alone:
Out of his bone a woman was made up
To share his joy, his table, and his cup.

Now he was happy,—happy as a clam—
And she was loving, gentle as a lamb,
And things looked well. He never dreamed that she
Would sell him out for apples on a tree,
Would load him down with trouble all his life,
And make him curse the day he took a wife;
That she would list to a beguiling snake,
Who'd snake 'em both into the burning lake.
Hard case for Adam, 'specially when he thought,
In single life, he'd ne'er have thus been caught,—
But lived forever in his loved retreat,
Without a care, except to pick and eat.

Third, Cain's exploits.   He was a farmer bred,
Achieved a fratricide at home, then fled
To Nod, near by, where long he wrought disorder,
And lived of old,—a ruffian of the border.
He was the first prize-fighter of his day;
Could whip his weight in wild cats, so they say.
The world waxed wicked.   Fourth, down poured the
        flood;
The waters rose till one poor wight, who stood
Knee-deep upon a mountain top, hail'd Noah,
And asked how soon the heavy shower'd be o'er?
"In forty days," the patriarch loud replied,
And, helm-a-port, veer'd off on 'tother side.
He left the wretch perched on the mountain peak,
Engulfed around, the wave up to his cheek,—
At which foul treatment there the man got mad,
And called the patriarch names uncouth and bad:
Old cove and hoax,—said forty days of rain
In one continuous spurt was humbug plain,
A thing unknown.   He b'lieved the wind would shift,
The rain hold up, and soon the fog would lift.

Then belching other billingsgate and *sass*
(Unfit for rhyme), said Noah might go to grass
With his big junk, crammed full of beasts and birds
And creeping things, caged in, in pairs and herds;
He'd take his chance alone,—he'd stan' his watch:
But hoped such heartless navigator'd catch
One of old Neptune's high, tempestuous wakers,
And get his great ark stranded on the breakers.

The deluge done, Noah sacrificed a lamb,
Got tipsy, too, 'fore Japheth, Shem, and Ham,
Kicked off his clothes, and did improper things,
Which shock my Muse, who blushes while she sings;
Cursed Ham and died,—a hard old dad was he,
Few would have cared if he had kept at sea.
Fifth, came confusion at the tower of Babel;
'Twas here the mother-tongue of Cain and Abel
Went out of use, and Hebrew, Latin, Greek,
High Dutch, and Fiji men in time did speak.
What followed then, how nations went astray
And built great cities, chiefly for display,
How wars broke out and ravaged those old times,
Would be too much for these most modest rhymes.
So, Muse, forbear.—This endeth the beginning.
Pray, don't you think my Pegasus is winning?

Methinks I hear some brother sigh: "Enough!
Dry up, O bard, on this old, mouldy stuff.
D'ye think we want to hear of Cain and Abel,
And hocus-pocus 'bout the tower of Babel
At this late day? Not much, I guess, dear sir!
You'd better take some topic we prefer,
The Tewksbury picture book, or Oscar Wilde,
Apostle Gove,—some dude more modern styled.

Oh, don't begin the world in getting started
Harping on chaps who have so long departed.''

A good suggestion, brother, timely made,
I'll profit by it and **make less** parade.
There won't be time, **I plainly** now perceive,
The whole **world's history to** rehearse this eve :
Besides, 'tis tiresome, and,—I'm getting dry,
Although, **my friends, a sober** man am I.
I'll shift **the scene, the** sentiment, **and meter,**
And **my staid Muse,** she shall be **now discreeter :**
And **while we shift, we'll let the** curtain *drap.*
An interlude just here to fill the gap
Methinks would come in well, and be the thing
To while the time, while we take higher wing.
If I permit the tide **of song** to drizzle,
I fear this Epic **may** turn out a fizzle.
Now for a space, **list** to the serenade :
The orchestra will **make** a little raid
With scientific music very brief.
Hark, **while** the minstrel sings : **" Hail to the Chief.''**

SONG.

[An **ancient** minstrel here steps out and sings an old version of " Hail to **the** Chief." He is accompanied by the full orchestra.]

All hail to **the** chief who in glory advancing,
Rides fearless and fast with a plume in his **cap :**
May the step of his charger, so valiantly prancing,
Quick answer the spur, and ne'er need a *huddap.*
Quick **answer the** spur, and ne'er need a *huddap.*

Hail, hail to the hero equipp'd and all ready
    To battle the foe, or to kneel to the fair :
Let him reap his reward in the smiles of some lady
    Who never will jilt him, or pull out his hair.
    Who never will jilt him, or pull out his hair.

A crown for the victor, of laurel and bay,
    A wreath for the lady so gentle and true ;
And for each at the altar a dainty bouquet,
    And a fig for Dan Cupid.—Sing, Halli-ba-loo !
    And a fig for Dan Cupid.—Sing, Halli-ba-loo !

SONG.

[The minstrel changes the key and sings " The Nut-Brown Maid."]

The nut-brown maid, in the gala masquerade,
    Was the one that befuddled me with wonder ;
Her eye was like a lance, as we tripp'd it thro' the dance,
    And she riddled my discretion all asunder.
    And she riddled my discretion all asunder.

Oh, the nut-brown maid, the cakes and lemonade,
    The music and the diamonds and the glitter,—
They were too much for me, I had to bend the knee
    To the maid with the cheek like a fritter.
    To the maid with the cheek like a fritter.

Since then I have a care, and I brace up like a bear
    When I see such a posy on the titter ;
And I never will again, be smash'd as I was then,
    By a maid with a cheek like a fritter.
    By a maid with a cheek like a fritter.

[At this point the bard having been properly **refreshed re-appears and with** becoming dignity resumeth his Epic.]

From dusty law-books what an awful **stride**
To that bright seat the beaming Muse **beside**!
A tall colossus scarce, methinks, **would take**
So huge a step, lest his long **legs should break**
And let him **down**, e'en with a grand careen,
Into **some wide and yawning** gulf between,—
Much less a novice. Pigmy legs and feet
Would quick give out, nor gain the blissful seat.

I heard a man say (**and it made me sad**,
And half I thought the foolish man **was mad**),
I heard him say, he b'lieved a lawyer's **tongue**
Was like a **trap**, bated ere it was sprung;
He b'lieved its hinge was somewhere 'bout **the middle**,
It wagg'd both ways, **its talk** was like a riddle;
That while on either side it would work splendid,
For honest truth that tongue was ne'er intended.
Confound **that man**, my indignation muttered!
A bigger lie no blackguard **ever** uttered.
He'd better move to some place **far away**,
Where fell attorneys do not prowl for prey;
He'll get, **if** caught about **the** court-house **sneaking**,
A plump *rebutter* for his evil speaking.

When my good brother rises in the court
Surcharged with law on contract, crime, or tort,
And **puts** the strong points noted on his brief,—
Somebody, sure, is bound to come to grief.
Now therefore, if, that is to say, now then,
If my **said** brother, speaking, where and when,
And so forth, should strain fearful hard to save
A desperate case,—shall **he be** called a knave?

Forbid it, Muse, tho' all the slanderers hiss you!
There's bread and butter pending on the issue.
Oh, never say he's talking just to win,
And for the merits does not care a pin;
But rather say his skill a marvel is,—
Exempli gratia, take a case like this:

A. versus B.—suit for a nine-tailed cat
B. bought of A. She caught full many a rat,
Was worth her price. But B. declines to pay
Because the cat, as he makes bold to say,
Had ten large tails, the which A. stout denies.
They join the issue which the court now tries.
Poor puss being dead herself they can't produce:
Besides, the witnesses are little use;
Their memory fails. Thus stands the contest when
B.'s lawyer rising argues for the ten.
Nine, says the plaintiff. *Ten*, B.'s counsel holds.
The which to prove his logic he unfolds
And argues thus: " No cat has nine tails, sure;
One cat has one: no truth than this is truer;
But one cat has more tails than no cat; then,
The plaintiff's cat you plainly see had ten."
The judge he listens, but no man can trace
His sound opinion on this knotty case.
'Twould be improper if he should let out
What he might think in such a case of doubt:
And if he should, nobody would be bound,
Because the law is all he can expound.
The jury's province 'tis, and aye hath been,
To find the facts. Sound argument will win.
Charged with the law on the disputed facts,
They now retire, and the shrewd foreman acts
As spokesman for the twelve: " It must be so.
A. has not made out half a case I know.

That argument is sound ; and I incline
To think that cat had one more tail than nine."
In which opinion they all coincide,
And by their verdict find the plaintiff lied.
Meantime B.'s lawyer walks about the bar
And shines resplendent as a new-made star,
While the outsiders laud him high, of course,
Saying, " Sir, he'd prove a dog's tail on a horse."

This is a tedious world, I sometimes think,
And far too many take to cards and drink ;
But something genial must be had to give
Our spirits zest, and cheer us while we live.
So fun is good.   What should we do without it?
The very world would rise in arms about it
Were it denied.   All Hades, too, would rattle
With gathering cohorts rushing forth to battle.
The air itself would be with brimstone tainted,
All damsels faint who'd not already fainted ;
Young men who go a wooing would despair,
Old baches grin and say they didn't care,—
The very beasts would growl and bite and wrangle
Were't not for fun this checkered life to spangle.

Youth is the season when the heart beats high
With bounding life, and joy lights up the eye ;
Youth is the season when young love first opes
Its fledgeling pinions, plumed with golden hopes.
Youth is the season and the gala day
When every youngster wants a sweetheart gay,
And every sweetheart dearly loves to mingle
In those bright scenes which set the heart a-jingle.
Youth is the season when we're bashful, too,
And bashful sprigs make always sad ado
In popping questions (which too early popped,
Were better checked, or by injunction stopped).

I've rode ten miles beside a pretty shawl
With heart quite full, yet could not speak at all;
And once I rode full twenty with a fair one,
Attired in white, ah me, she was a rare one!
And in an absent-minded fit, I let
My horse dash thro' a slough of miry wet,
Which so bespattered her bright form, that she
Cast withering glances all the way at me.
Youth is the season,—but I'll here hold in:
To tell the whole would be, perhaps, a sin,
'Twould never do; and I should rather perish
Than compromise the flames I used to cherish.

Oh, Robert Burns! How do my verses vary!
Those pretty lines you wrote your Highland Mary
Who went to heaven,—did always seem to me
To make it strange you could a drunkard be.
Your heart was tender and your soul alive,
And when your rustic plowshare once did drive
A mousie out, or turned the mountain daisy,
You stopped to rhyme,—for which the world long
    praise ye!
Oh, Robert Burns, why were you e'er so wayward!
Alas, 'tis pity cause there was to say word
Against your wild, yet most bewitching nature,—
Cause to lament you were so weak a creature.
But gifted men of noble heart and head,
Full oft " the primrose path of dalliance " tread;
And some go over to a swift perdition,
And ere life's zenith end their earthly mission.

This Epic soon must close. Let me pass on.
There is a thing that once was in the ton
And still hath many very curious uses,
And oftentimes sensation deep produces.

7

That thing is whalebone, which when I was small
I used to get and hate the worst of all.
'Twas once, indeed, the staple of the market,
And I myself did rather like than shirk it:
It made the straight skirts stand out so bewitching,—
I used to think I should not fear a switching
If such a shield I had around my spindles,—
A thing which still my admiration kindles.
I used to think the whalebone made the style:
I told the girls, when they did laugh and smile,
That I predicted gents would use it soon,
Either to raise their coat tails to the moon,
Or else to make a lattice work of arches,
Whereon to train their glorious, long moustaches.
I used to tell 'em whales were getting scarce,
They'd soon play out, but *bone* was ne'er a farce.
That flesh and bone would long go well together;
But solid meat would sure outweigh a feather.
Told them the stuff, tho' somewhat hard to burn up,
Was good to keep. Some new device would turn up,
And new devices always pleased the ladies,
Ere Lucy spoke, or Barnum thought of babies.
I could not close these grand, heroic verses
Without this tribute to that source of curses
Which pestered me when I was young and playful,
And took the girls out riding by the shay-full.

Here this grand Epic ends. *Nunc vates exit:*
Exeunt omnes; carmen magnum rexit:
Which is a modest, classic way of saying,
The bard retires, since he has done his braying.
The crowd go home. This verse, like Fogg's philippic,
Hath had its day. Selah! *Et vale*, Epic!

THAT SUMMER HAT.

'Twas the coquettish month of May,—
  I saw a man go down the street
In winter clothes, save on his head
    A panama, quite new and neat,
    As if to vent some surplus heat.

I watched that man go down the street,—
  'Twas early in the afternoon:
I half inclined to counsel him;
    Friend, you are out a month too soon,
    Pray, save that summer hat till June.

But fearing he might say to me,
  What business is it, sir, to you?
I let him pass without a word;
    But still the hat so nice and new
    Somehow my gaze intently drew.

Most of the hats 'twere out that day
  Were winter hats, that held the heat;
I could not guess why this one man,
    With winter costume else complete,
    Should sport his pan'ma on the street.

He elbowed thro' the jostling crowd,
  Conspicuous by his shining brim;
I trembled lest some surly gust
    (He was a man so tall and slim)
    Should make a laughing stock o' him.

For this coquettish **month of May,**
     So full of pranks, **is such a shrew,**
She nips us even when she smiles.
     Beware of her bright sunshine, **you,**
     Who **sport** sombreros nice and new.

Behold, **my** friend hath made a pause ;
     And o'er the spirit of his dream
Hath come a change !   I saw as 'twere,
     In broad daylight, **a meteor gleam,**
     And heard some dozen urchins **scream.**

There was a chase far down the street,
     The wayward **hat kept** well ahead ;
At times my friend **a point did make,**
     Then veer'd the hat and onward sped
     Till, " drat the thing !" half mad he said.

Which is the reason why 'twon't do,
     In this coquettish month of May,
To sport a pau'ma brimm'd so wide
     Upon the street.   Wherefore I say,
     " Friend, keep it for a later day."

THE TWO ST. PATRICKS.

JOHN DALEY, THE STHRAME OVER:

AN' HOW HE SAW THE TWA ST. PATRICKS.

[The late Dr. Ezekiel Holmes of Winthrop, for many years editor of the *Maine Farmer*, prefaced a version of the following poem published in his paper in the life-time of its subject, with the following paragraph, viz.:

"Our neighbors in W. are well acquainted with that *gin-a-wine* Hibernian, 'Sprig of Shillalah,' Johnny O'Daley, all the way from 'Baillie James Duff in the Emerald Isle,'—social, good-natured, and witty when sober, but quarrelsome and '*orfully* rantankerous' when the 'craithure is in him.' His mad pranks when in the latter situation are the cause oftentimes for his finding quarters in the House of Correction, which he humorously calls the 'Orthodox Jail.' Och! but he's a broth of a boy."]

Who lives jist below by the bend o' the sthrame?
    Troth, who but John Daley himsel';
Wi' the brogue o' the bog on his rattlesome tongue,
An' his mischief o' wit as he whistles along,—
    This neighborhood knows him full well.

John Daley, ye're chip o' a thrue Irish block,
    An' ye dhraws as an Irishman can,
Contintment an' paice frae the pipe that ye smoke;
Ye quarrels sometimes, but more often ye joke
    Like the happiest man in the lan'.

No doubt ye dug ditches lang syne in Connaught,
    An' thought na' the toil was a burthen:
The skill that ye ha', man, in work o' that kind
Wud lave a sprawl Yankee tin paces behind
    In threnchin' a gintleman's garthen.

I've ne'er heard ye boast o' good looks for yersel',
 Nor compliment do the owld ledthy;
But the childer ye used to extol to the skies,
Saying: "Darlints more han'some ne'er winked their bright
  eyes,
 Nor ga' one a smile ha' so predthy."

D'ye mind the owld pistol ye call'd Watherloo?
 The one ye kep' loa'thed, ye said,
To dhrive frae yer house the too troublesome beaux,—
Ah! cruel John Daley to dhrive off the beaux,
 Despite ye yer daughters have wed.

There's one thing I grieve,—ye sometimes dhrink grog:
 Ye act like the de'il, as they tell,
When ye dhrink to excess,—ye're defiant o' men,
An' ye seem like a wild, ranting lunatic then,
 An' niver John Daley himsel'.

Why d'ye do it, owld boy? I doubt na' ofttimes,
 Ye ha' thought that the Orthodox Jail
Was na' place for a son o' the Emerald Isle,—
Yer pious godfather, d'ye think he wud smile
 To see ye mew'd up in its pale?

In penance ye vowed not to taste it again:
 Ye'd sooner cut off the owld han',
Whose fingers were blawn to the winds,—save a stub,
Left for loa'thin' the pipe an' definse in a rub,—
 Ye'd show 'em John Daley could stan'.

Why was it, my hearty, ye missed it so oft
 When rollickin' free and at large?
Were yer good resolutions entirely forgot,
That ye slipp'd an' went off on yer beer ere ye thought,
 An' again for the jail were a charge?

Was't the toothache that did it,—the toothache, that once
    Took ye sore in the jaw, as ye said,
An' they gae ye a spoonful o' grog for the pain,
Which ye held in yer mouth (till ye swallowed again),
    Long ago, when a wild Irish blade?

How oft ha' I heard ye speak up for the faith
    In serious,—no joking—no fun:
An' hould that the church (gie St. Peter the glory!)
Goes back thro' the ages primeval an' hoary
    As far as the light 'o the sun.

" Yis, an' farther," ye said, " else did niver John Daley
    Spake thrue o' the things that he wot of;
Six thousand long years lived the church an' saved sowls
Ere the heretic Luther ran off frae the faul's,
    Or a Protistint Bible was thought of.''

I've in mind an owld sthory ye tell o' the days
    When ye bowed like a saint to the cross
In the blissed owld counthry, far over the wave,
Reptile-purged by St. Patrick (his relics God save!
    Not a bone o' thim knows of a loss).

How in a cathedral, whose dim-lighted arches
    Smilt howly of incense an' praise,
Down stairs ye once went wi' the praist an' a candle,
An' he said ye might see, but forbid ye to handle,
    Bones o' saints who'd long numbered their days.

An' a sthrappan big door he unbolted an' swung,
    Whin ye saw wi' amazement an' dread,
A dhry skeleton standin' eight foot in his cell,
Every bone in its place an' adjusted so well,
    That the craithure, he hardly seem'd dead.

" Who is it?" quo' John : " None else," said the praist,
  " Than St. Patrick whose name we revere."
So he left the big door an' led on wi' the light
To a nate little cupboard jist 'round to the right,
  Which he opened, saying : " Now, man, look here."

An' ye looked in an' saw 'twas the bones of a child,
  Standin' jist to yer waist, as ye said ;
All perfect an' comely frae toe bone to skull,—
An eye like a mouse hole, wi' mischief as full,
  Lookin' less than the ither like dead.

" An' who's this?" quo' John : an' the praist made reply :
  " 'Tis St. Patrick long gone to his joy."
" Twa St. Patricks?" cried John ; said the praist : " under-
     stan',
The first that ye saw was St. Patrick, the man,
  An' this is St. Patrick, the boy."

Long live ye, John Daley, jist down by the sthrame,
  Crack jokes, if ye will, till ye die ;
Kape sober an' scape frae the Orthodox Jail,
Make the balance o' life but a holiday sail,
  Ye'll be wanted elsewhere by and by.

Some day in the gloamin' ye'll go o'er the sthrame.
  An' ye'll niver come back to yer door ;
For yer whistlin' an' jokes folks'll listen in vain,
An' the songs that ye sing in a high, merry strain
  Will be heard by the neighbors no more.

But far be the day ! An' the meadows grow green
  While ye tenant the house by the bend.
Shure, the patch on the sthrame where the best pratees grow
Will miss ye o'ermuch when ye pass from the show
  An' yer holiday life to an end.

HOW IT HAPPENED:

A RHYME EXPLANATORY FOR JOHN DALEY.

I ha' heard John Daley, ye'd jist like to know
  Who rhymed ye so free in the paper
Without yer consint an' towld rascally lies,—
How the wag, if ye caught him, ye'd gie him black eyes
  To pay for that impudint caper.

Ye'd gie him black eyes?   Fie, fie, what a man,
  When a joker ye are yer own sel';
Now away wi' such talk an' yer passions control:
Come, gie us yer han' an' I'll tell ye the whole,
  So ye'll know how that mischief befel.

Ye see 'twas one night in a dhrame that I had,
  I was walking jist down by the sthrame,
When divers loud voices I heard in the sky,
An', sudden, ten rhymers like goblins went by,
  Shouting: "Johnny O' Daley for fame!"

An' they rode all along by the banks o' the sthrame,
  An' belaguered John's premises 'round:
From the Dead House the Shanghais gae forth in dismay
Such a screech as the very old Nick were to pay
  Nor a bit o' hot pitch to be found.

An' the rhymers gave orders: " John Daley, come forth ! "
    Not afeard, but reluctant was John :
So they bolted right in, took him out o' his bed,
Dressed him up in his clothes, put a hat on his head,
    Brought a horse, an' they bade him get on.

Then the man who'd " not knuckle to St. Peter himsel',"
    He mounted that nag in a minute :
Saying, " Shure, its not I to refuse a good ride,—
The baste is as fine as one nade to bestride,
    An' I'll go tho' the mischief be in it."

An' the rhymers all laughed: " Ha, ha, ha, he's good
      pluck,
    He's worthy as Cæsar of fame :
So we'll take him along without squabble or strife,
An' we'll print all the things he e'er did in his life,
    Since they called him John Daley by name.

" We'll tell of his pranks, an' his wit, an' his fun,
    Of his pipe of contintmint an' paice,
Of his Watherloo pistol which killed a man dead,
An' his fingerless han' a Philistine might dread,
    If he caught the dhry knock in his face.

" An' we'll tell how he saw the dhry bones o' the two,—
    St. Patrick the man an' the boy—
In the blissed owld counthry, ere he sailed all the way
From Baillie James Duff to the St. Lawrence Bay
    In the immigrant craft, Ship-a-hoy.

" For the world ought to know o' these wonderful things ;
    An' the world would laugh hearty no doubt,
If it kenn'd but the half what he's said an' he's done.
There's a prank he once played both for freedom an' fun
    Which the doctors might tell for the gout.

" The story goes thus : John Daley once lodged
  Over night in the Orthodox Jail,
Quite elastic, indade, but not out o' his wits :
'Twas in times when Maine Law gae the rumsellers fits
  Upon proof of unauthorized sale.

" Next day to that jail went the strict selectman,
  All zeal in the temperance strife :
' 'Tis a sorrowful sight, John, to see ye in here ;
If I thought ye'd behave an' the facts could appear,
  I'd let ye go home to yer wife.'

" John promised full well an' strong facts did disclose,
  Showing plain 'twas one Packard made sale :
Said he had grog o' him an' gae *tin* for it too,
An' he'd swear it in court if they'd jist put him thro',
  An' John could go forth from the jail.

" So John was released an' next day in the court
  Swore the truth, like a witness demure :
' Had ye grog o' this Packard arraigned on complaint?'
' Yis, I had.' ' Did ye pay for it? ' ' Niver a cint,
  I did not, now, Yer Honor, be shure.'

" Then the lawyer so smart : ' Do ye mean to say that?
  What, did ye not tell the s'lectman
Ye had grog o' this Packard an' gave him the *tin?*'
' Ah, Yer Honors, I did : 'Twas to put the grog in,
  Shure, the *tin* was me little tin can.' "

An' the rhymers kept talking these things to themselves :
  " Yes, an' there was the journey he made
To Kintuck wi' one Hammond, both back in dispair,
Being too abolition to suit 'em out there,
  An' suspected perhaps of a raid."

An' the rest o' the things, the back bone o' John's fame,
  All in detail they said should appear :
Henceforth wi' the big bugs he'd be an' the kings,
His name in the corners o' papers where sings
  The Muse like a brisk chanticleer.

Here the rhymers pranced off wi' the haro along,
  An' were soon wi' the darkness begrimed :
I saw them no more ; but the paper next day
Had a scrap in the corner,—an' that was the way
  John Daley, the dabster, was rhymed.

ODE FOR THE X. Y. Z.

[A literary society which had been much interested in the reading of Huc's travels in Tartary.]

An ode then it is for this Thanksgiving eve.
    Pray what shall its character be?
Not silly, not sad, for both would be bad
    In the tastes of the X. Y. Z.

Something neat but not gaudy, it strikes me would do;
    Something.—ah, it's right in my eye,
So, Peggy, go long,—what, do your visions throng
    But with manes of puddings and pie?

In sooth if they do, not worse are you off
    Than I, your unfortunate master:
The good things of life must sometimes be rife,
    In the brain of a young poetaster.

But go long, sir, I say: go faster along!
    There's nor reason nor rhyme in delay:
Flap smartly your wings, for astonishing things
    Must be done on this festival day.

There, better, *eclat!* You gain on it now.
    But stop, let me speak to my Nancy,
That everything pretty to weave in a ditty
    May come in a trice to my fancy.

Who's she, is it asked? Why, a genius of thought.
    There's one for every true poet:
Mine I call Nancy for her necromancy
    'S my *sine qua non* of go it.

Starting fair then, with aid of both Nancy and Peg,
  We're off for a metrical jingle :
Right merry good sense, unreserved we'll dispense
  To you all both married and single.

First greet we the fair ones, since chiefly to them
  Indebted, O brothers, are we,
For this chance of reciting our excellent writing,
  And showing what pumpkins we be.

Oh, may they be happy! (as also may we!)
  Inasmuch as they've had their own way :
But to sit here and listen when genius might glisten
  Is not the fair thing, I should say.

Well, fair ones all greeted, we now pass on
  To the poetry part of our ode,
Which, if I survive to the end, I shall strive
  To finish up quite *a la mode*.

Come, pretty conceits, that always will come,
  At the call of the lyrical bard :
Come, fashion my rhyme, make it tall and sublime
  Like the won'erful camelopard.

Natural history I like, hence similes drawn
  From that source always give me great pleasure :
Two or three more, like the one just before,
  Would make these verses a treasure.

But this is digression, so all out of place :
  What follows hereafter shall be
Pure poetry, such as I seldom shall touch
  With the brush of my *jeu d' esprit*.

Be cautious, my Peggy, we fly very high ;
    Look out for the stars as you go,
Keep clear of Orion and Leo, the lion,
    And all those fellows you know.

How glibly we glide thro' the regions of space !
    I seldom have gone it like this
The earth way below, like a vagabond crow,
    Seems wandering 'round the abyss.

My ! what a flurry of beautiful thoughts
    Were those that flew past me then,—
Ah, were it not that there's a brick in my hat
    I should have dismounted been !

Hold ! others I see, but emaciate they look
    And thin as the ghost of a sinner :
They're nothing, by dickens, but shades of those chickens
    We had in a pie for dinner.

What's yonder out there ? My stars, 'tis a comet,
    I know by this sulphurous smell :
Now if we should fail to keep clear of his tail
    We may go where the blue devils dwell.

Let's return then, forthwith, without any delay
    No further up here will I roam.
The world I still see—oh, thither let's flee,
    And won't it seem good to get home?

Welcome, ye regions familiar once more !
    We're grateful as grateful can be :
But before we alight, we'll take a short flight,
    The land of the Tartars to see.

A fine country this !   Nice people are these,—
  As pretty a place as I've been in !
The lamas look sleek, the camels look meek,
  Not slow the Mongolian women.

Here's one chap I know.   'Tis Samdad-Schiem,
  The friend of my friend, Mr. Huc :
I've seen him quite oft, his head's rather soft,
  But still he's a man of good pluck.

Lo, what do they here on the bank of the river?
  They're casting out spirits, I guess ;
For men never I've known so a hill to run down,—
  Why, what does their senses possess?

Ha, I see thro' it now !   No longer to tell
  What they're up to I am at a loss.
They all go ker-thump on the old camel's rump,
  And thus they propel him across.

Having seen all that's here, we'll now go back,
  And make preparations to stop,—
Not rashly, indeed, but we'll break off our speed
  After something the style of a top.

Which you know always stops when it goes very fast,
  By gradually ceasing to whirl ;
So a verse or two more and the cry of *encore*
  Unheeding, our pinions we'll furl.

Before closing I ought very truly to say
  What music I meant should be used
In singing these lines.   My fancy opines
  The music should not be confused.

For good lines are oft spoilt by bad music you know,
    As new bottles are burst by old wine :
Now I should be sorry to stop in such hurry
    As not to have music divine.

I shan't do it. I shall try, tho' vainly I try,
    To select for these verses a song :
The Muse I will at her to help in this matter,
    The meter I think I'll have long ;

Unless particular 'd better convey
    The meaning and sense of my rhyme :
If 'twould, then say I, by all means, let's try
    Particular meter this time.

Fie ! I can't sing alone : for if I don't hear
    A voice in the treble I'm dumb.
Oh, would that some *Annie*, with voice sweet as manna,
    Would help me, we'd then give it some !

But 'tis vain. Besides, I'm too tired just now
    To arrange a good song for my verses :
So sing as you like 'em, dear sirens, don't spite 'em,
    Try 'em on when the choir rehearses.

Now stop I right here. I've determined on this :
    You couldn't persuade me to go
A page further for money, no, nor even for honey,
    Both which I like well as you know.

So hush'd be the lute strings ! Rest thee, my Peg,
    Best beast that was ever bestrode !
Here's verse thirty-four and never a one more,
    And this is the end of our ode.

THE GOVERNOR.

GOV. DUNN'S NEW HAT.

[Presented to him at the January Term, 1881, by the Androscoggin Bar Association.]

The ancient tile which late he wore
They say was nobby years before,
    When he was Gov.,
But on it for the last decade
Have blight and mildew sorely preyed;
'Tis all unfit for dress parade,
    Put 't in the stove.

For in its place a stylish one,
Bang up and shining as a bun,
    He now supports ;
It sits majestic on his pow,
And shelters his Websterian brow,—
No better-looking lawyer now
    Frequents the courts.

Keep still about the boots and coat
And stand-up collar round his throat ;
    We can afford
To tolerate such dress as that,—
We won't except to his cravat :
What we complained of was the hat.
    Say not a word.

I know the old one somehow took :
It had a good old Bourbon look,
    Till fusion struck ;
Then, like a greenback soiled and rent,
All of a sudden it was spent,
And with its substance, some say, went
    Jacksonian pluck.

But that is an aspersion foul,
At which the Gov'nor'll raise a howl.
    Shade of A. J. !
Forbid that e'er a son of thine,
Who'd thus his loyalty resign,
Should have a hat wherewith to shine !
    How's that for high?

Now, David, take us in to lunch,
And give us lemonade or punch,—
        Something to cheer;
For we are down i' th' mouth to-day:
Our gentle Swan has fled away,—
Gone where the woodbine twines, they say,
        When wanted here.

Gone to the prairies, all forlorn,
A sharp'ning scythes and shelling corn,—
        Whisper it low.
Why did he leave us on the sly,
Nor stop to bid the Bar good-by?
Who *bribed* him to desert and fly?
        Tell if you know.

THE WATER CAMPAIGN IN AUBURN,

MARCH, 1882.

A thoughtful man went home at night
　　Revolving in his mind:
What if the city should burn up
　　Nor leave a trace behind?

What if the fire fiend should break loose,
　　Run riot round the town,
And singe the whiskers off my cheeks,
　　The hair from off my crown?

Who'd have to bear the blame for this,
　　When right beneath our feet,
Protection flows in iron pipes,
　　So ample and complete?

I own no stock; I only take
　　My water straight and plain,
And pay my taxes like a man, —
　　Lord! what have I to gain?

I lie awake all night for fear;
　　I raise no points of law:
The contract gave the city, sure,
　　A perfect right to draw,

And that's enough. 'Who bust that trade,
　　And left us all exposed
To fire and brimstone? Let the scamps'
　　Foul mischief be disclosed.

We'll rout this city government,
　　And stop this foul misrule ;
We'll put in men who money have,—
　　None of **your** poll-tax school ;

We'll send the lunk-heads home at once,
　　And have some *statesmen* who
Will see the one important thing,—
　　Protect both me and you ;

And when our little job is done,
　　Our *coup d'élat* attained,
We'll quietly disband and go
　　Our several **ways** unstained.

There is no treason in our acts,
　　No *Gile* within our hearts ;
Gile does not play a part with us,
　　Be-*Giling* with sly arts.

We're *Gileless* all as bleating lambs ;
　　But when our backs **is up**
We fight for right with Spartan pluck,
　　And ne'er the cudgel drop.

When, in **the course of** town affairs,
　　A crisis comes like this,
We fuse and rally one and all,—
　　No matter how they hiss.

So rally, voters, rank and **file,**
　　Throw off all party ties :
Protection **is the** thing we **want,**
　　The apple **of** our eyes.

Clean out the poll-tax men who rule,—
    Throw dust and dirt and gravel;
Don't let them make our *Jordan* road
    A hard, hard road to travel.

James Dingley's grievance is severe,
    His wrongs cry for redress;
And, by the great horn-spoon, we'll give
    This poll-tax crowd distress.

And, when the hash is settled up,
    A love-feast we will hold,
And generations now unborn
    Will laugh when this is told.

JENKINS.

TO JENKINS, THE JANITOR.

You asked me, Jenkins, 'bout the book,
    How soon 'twas going to issue?
And I mistrusted from your look
    You thought you'd like its tissue.

You told me, Jenkins, you'd subscribe
    And buy one, if I'd print 'em;
You'd help me out, my health imbibe
    When I abroad had sent 'em.

I put you down among my friends,—
    A whole-soul'd, generous fellow;
A man of taste, who comprehends
    The deep thoughts and the shallow.

The Court-House is your special care,
    You keep the furnace sighing,
You bring the books for lawyers there,
    You watch the cases trying.

You fetch the Judge his daily mail,
    You wait upon the ladies,
Who crowd the galleries to the rail,
    Tho' foul the air as Hades;

(This last is not a fault of yours:
    No court-room will smell fragrant,
But gaseous, like the slums and sewers,
    When comes the crowd so vagrant.)

You brush up the attorneys' room,
    And try to keep it tidy:
But still, in spite of brush and broom,
    Some make it look like hidy.

That room has got a checker-board,
    I see, that's used by many:
If now at law we're skunk'd and floor'd,
    We'll have a game, I vanny.

The table has no Bible yet,
    Tho' soon I hope to note it:
Here's missionary field, you bet,
    And heathen who can't quote it.

I answer you, my friend, in rhyme,
    Tho' further I sha'n't spin it:
The book will issue in due time,
    And, Jenkins, you'll be in it.

JUDGE WALTON'S THERMOMETER.

Some judges on the bench give weighty thought
To points of law, as learned judges ought;
And ne'er rouse up, tho' sweltering with the heat,
Or shivering cold with icy hands and feet.

Some keep the law all straight and still take care
To have the court-room flushed with good fresh air,
To have the temperature kept at the point
Where mind and muscle won't get out of joint.

Our Judge, while gracing well the bench supreme,
Allows no trifling with his favorite scheme:
If 'tis too hot, too cold,—if aught's amiss,
Up goes his finger, " Jenkins, see to this !"

He knows what's right: and for his certain guide
He's got an instrument that is his pride,
Which he hangs up where it is full in view,
So he can see, and Jenkins can see too.

And it is just one marvelous little thing,
With figures on it, and on top a ring
To hang it up by, and the mercury goes
So curious thro' the long, glass tube it shows.

The proper court-room gauge upon the face
Of this judicial toy,—the stopping place,
Sine qua non—is seventy in the shade :
The mercury here, the Judge ne'er makes a raid.

But let it mount up, say, to eighty-five,
The Judge and Jenkins scarcely would survive ;
The lawyers roast,—and prematurely some
Might catch a foretaste of the doom to come.

If any, fore-ordained to burn by'n by
In the great pit where furnace heat runs high,
Should seize that thing when stepping off the stage,—
Who knows but *there* 'twould fix the court-room gauge :

Toning the heat down to that standard which
Would be congenial in the lawyers' niche ;
Clearing from smoke the surcharged, sultry air,
Making the brimstone fumes less pungent there?

GEN. BUTLER APPEARS FOR THE LASTERS.

[S. J. C., AND. CO., APRIL TERM, 1884.—HASKELL, J., PRESIDING.]

Nunc " *mons laboravit et.*"—*mirabile dictu!*
The prettiest little fable Uncle Æsop ever knew ;
One chock-full of Latin, and chock-full of sense,—
There's nothing like a big gun to muster for defense.
Hearken how the General himself came down
And answered for the laster-men here in Auburn town.

The case called in order, he riz up in the court,
Said his clients all were innocent as little lambs at sport ;
Said they didn't break the law (but trial he would waive),
And they'd promise for the future to be civil and behave ;
Said they'd never re-assemble the workers to combat,—
The case might hang along as a guaranty for that.

Defense was very brief : but the people they came out
For to hear and for to see what the Gen'ral was about :
Some said the State's attorney, why, he'd floor him on the sly,
And never raise his finger or even cock his eye.
It transcended all the Barnum shows that ever yet came 'roun',
The Gen'ral with the Glover Band to 'scort him thro' the town.

From city and from suburb, the women and the men,
Came thronging to the trial,—all who'd ever heard of Ben :
They waited on the steps and they jostled and they jamm'd,
And when the court was opened, the court-room it was
        cramm'd.
They listened and they gazed with an interest most intense,
But couldn't see nor hear at all the crowd was so immense.

The talk was to his Honor there, and when the talk was done,
They thought the great defense, forsooth, had not in fact
      begun ;
And they were mad as hoppers and were disappointed sore
When told the great defense, forsooth, was finished and all
      o'er.
Some hadn't seen the General and vowed they'd not go
      home ;
Some swore 'twas all a blarsted sell and wish'd they hadn't
      come.

One laster didn't like the terms agreed to in defense
And claimed his right to trial there indicted for offense ;
And refusing to recognize for appearance at the next,
Was chuck'd into the jail awhile, dumfoundered and per-
      plexed ;
But fifteen minutes' durance vile repented him, and he
Recognized with the rest and said : " Jail is no place for
      me ! "

The upshot of it all was this, achieved by skill sublime,
Not a single striking laster was convicted of the crime ;
The Gen'ral clear'd them all at once, by tactics shrewd and
      brave,
On condition and providin' they'd remember to behave :
Which was glorious for the Gen'ral and for the lasters too,
And a gala day for Auburn town I here remark to you.

The Gen'ral beats the world you see.   He plays his card to
      win,
And mighty smart must be the man who takes the Gen'ral in :
He missed it once in Tewksbury, but pray now what o' tha'?
His victory here will make amends and give him great *eclat.*
But blaze it not in Tewksbury, for they don't like to hear,—
Such glory for the General would nettle them I fear.

THE AUBURN GHOST.

[A few years ago, while a revival was in progress in Auburn, an apparition appeared on several occasions, and created quite a sensation in town. The following poem, written at that time, commemorates the experience of a young man who encountered the mysterious presence on his way home from evening meeting. The facts are, substantially, as vouched for by him. The moral is simply a suggestion, showing the danger of too many sweethearts on the arm at one and the same time.]

Now, when the work o' grace is doin',
And many sinners are eschewin'
Their wicked ways,—pray, what's a brewin'?
      Beelzebub
Is plotting mischief, fright, an' ruin,
      Their faith to snub.

They cannot keep him chained an' bound;
Still, as of old, he's bummin' 'round
All pious counsels to confound:
      His horn an' hoof
From scarce one spot o' hallow'd ground
      Will keep aloof.

Sometimes in black, sometimes in white,
Disguised, he stalks in broad daylight;
An' sometimes prowlin' late at night,
      'Bout ten or 'leven,
He waylays meetin' folks,—to fright
      Their souls from heaven.

Seldom he tackles old an' tried ones,
Who, steadfast as the glorified ones,
Stand firm, howe'er the evil tide runs :
          He chooses rather
The tender converts, young, bright-eyed ones,
          To scare an' bother.

Last Monday night, when dim the moon
Thro' misty clouds scarce blinked aboon,
A young man, hummin' sacred tune,
          Goin' home from meetin'
With Misses three, fell in a swoon
          At his rough greetin'.

He first smelled brimstone, then he saw
Old Nick's grim beldam near 'em draw
With one long-jointed, harpy claw
          Outstretched to grab 'em,
An' teeth set in a lantern jaw,
          Sharp filed, to nab 'em.

Full eight feet high, the young man said,
At them the specter shook its head
With eyeballs glaring fiery red,
          Then belched a groan,
Whereat the damsels screamed an' fled,
          An' he fell down,

So terror-stricken an' unmanned,
He could not raise his valiant hand
Against the foe, nor make a stand,—
          But lay there dyin',
Without one thought o' happy land,
          Or damsels flyin'.

9

Now thank the Lord, whose power arose
Right here against foul fiends **an'** foes
An' saved his lambs!   **Alas, who knows**
　　　　How dire the harm,
Had he forgot to interpose
　　　　His strong right arm?

Ah, what a frightful tale to tell
Had old Nick caught each bloomin' belle,—
Had three been seized in that brief spell
　　　　By art satanic,
An' hurried, sudden, off to hell—
　　　　Oh, what a panic!

MORAL.

Young **man!** young man! **when late at night**
The meetin's out, **an'** all the light
Is Auburn's gas, not extra bright,
　　　　Escort **but one;**
Take never three, lest you take fright
　　　　An' be undone!

FINALE.

The show is over. Here the curtain falls:
You need not hearken now for caterwauls,—
'Tis past midnight and all the cats have fled.
This orchestra is tired and going to bed.

Confound the Muses! I ejaculate:
Nunc libera me! They'd keep one on the wake
Till lights burn blue, when one should snoring be,
Not out with them larking it merrily.

Confound them all! No sober, married man
Should flirt with them. He'd better, if he can,
Drive them to roost at early candle-light:
They murder sleep, if they get out at night.

Then when at morn one hears the bantam crow,
He will wake up with vigorous life aglow:
Not look blear-eyed, like votaries at the shrine
Of ancient maids yclept the Sacred Nine.

Considerate bards at night hang up the lyre,
And quench awhile the wild, Promethean fire.
I follow suit, and with the poker bury
The embers deep, for I feel prosy, very.

The show is done. Now scatter and disperse!
You will not get from me another verse:
Grave doubts still haunt me as when I begun,
But I shall rally, now the concert's done.

OCCASIONAL POEMS.

The foregoing, it is believed, embraces the "effusions" called for by the vote of the Bar Association, and completes the collection intended to be included under the title, "INSIDE THE BAR."

At the suggestion and request of some friends, and with the approval of the Association I believe, I publish in this connection a few poems of a different character, some of early date, others more recent, several of which are quite outside the legal atmosphere. I need offer no apology here, I think, for these additions to the collection. Whether to couple them with what precedes is strictly in accordance with good taste and that nice sense of propriety which should be observed by one venturing before the public in work of this kind, those who read must judge. If the occasional poems which follow possess any interest, local, personal, or otherwise, for those into whose hands the book may fall, and are not distasteful to the members of our fraternity, it may perhaps be deemed a sufficient warrant for introducing them here.

J. W M.

THE BURDEN OF THE RHYME.

I want a burden, one that I can carry,
  An easy, tasteful burden for my rhyme:
A yielding mass which I can shape and vary.
  And fashion to my whim at any time.

I want a burden,—not a cumbrous weight,
  To weigh me down whene'er I spread a wing,
And force my lyre to cries disconsolate,
  When I, forsooth, should like a syren sing:—

No pilgrim's pack, but just a well-poised load,
  Which I can swing with an elastic tread,—
One that shall not my freedom incommode,
  While on I press to gain the prize ahead.

I want,—what do I want? 'Twere sweet to know
  One's pressing want in such an hour of need.
'Tis not a legend with romance aglow,
  'Tis not a warrior prancing on his steed,

'Tis not a hero. These are commonplace
  And crowd before us whereso'er we go.
'Tis something nameless my mind's eye would trace
  And which I fain would spread before you now.

For I have wandered in some pleasant fields,
　　By cool cascades, in pathways where the sun
A mellow radiance thro' green foliage yields,
　　And soft, responsive voices, many a one,

Have whispered me, unheard by other ears ;
　　And strains of music such as only come
From sources where one sees no form, but hears
　　Eolian murmurings as his footsteps roam ;—

Such marvelous strains at times mine ear hath caught,
　　And I have listened till the music's spell
Within my soul an ecstasy hath wrought,
　　Such as no earthly minstrel can compel.

It is not all a witch note of the air,
　　The fitful trembling of some wild harp-strings,
That wins me thus and chains my spirit there,
　　As to a fount whence inspiration springs.

Not in such fields and pathways of delight
　　The burden of the poet's song is found :
Nor from such sources, fanciful and bright,
　　Issue the rhythmic measures of sweet sound.

The burden of the poet's living song
　　Lies not in theme or net-work of a lay :
The theme is stale,—unless 'tis borne along
　　By flood of melody that must have way.

The ringing note, the echo lingering sweet,
　　The breathing word whose utterance thrills the heart,
The earnest thought that doth itself repeat,
　　The tender touch that bids the tear to start,

The flow of numbers gathering force and fire,
    The stress of song impatient of control,—
These are the burden of the poet's lyre,
    Springing harmonious from his inmost soul.

Therefore if something of that magic power
    Shall stir within, I shall the burden find;
Nor, haply, lack the skill for one brief hour
    To sway some heart responsively inclined.

Therefore I yield at times, and softly touch
    The harp whose strings are with the ivy clad:
Tho' my vain effort miss the mark o'ermuch,
    Yet I rejoice if but one heart is glad.

WEST PITCH.

WEST PITCH.

[The falls at the Androscoggin at Lewiston, Me., are divided by a high pro-jection of the ledge, between which and the Auburn side is a deep gorge or channel worn through the rock, and known as West Pitch. In time of freshet the great body of the water passes down through this gorge, presenting a grand spectacle and constituting the most interesting feature of the falls.]

List to the sound of the cataract's roar!
That deep-toned voice you have heard before,
It hath spoken for ages—its thundering tongue
Is ever attuned to the same old song.

It speaks when the spring-time floods come down,
As the ocean speaks when tempests frown;
Then dies away as the summer comes
To a lullaby soft as the rivulet hums.

See how the waters first pause on the brink,
As if from the terrible plunge they would shrink,
Then shudder and curl—till over they go
Like an avalanche hurled on the rocks below;

Sending wreaths of foam and spray afar,
In the clash of their elemental war;
While up from the boiling tumult leaps
A cloud in whose mists a rainbow sleeps.

Stand on the shelf of the rifted rock,
Where the current goes down with a whirl and a shock,—
Tumultuous, wild, impetuous, grand,
With a might no barrier can now withstand:

Gaze on that hell with suspended breath—
Think of the suicides' terrible death.
And the fiercer hell of the heart which hurled
The victims, ruthlessly, out of the world.

Ah, what a burden comes now on the song!
List to the howl which the waters prolong:
Two poor wretches,—frail, maidenly forms,
Together o'erwhelmed in the cataract's arms.

Speak not of errors which sicken the heart
And madden the brain till reason depart—
Your voice, O frenzied waters, to-day
Is a demon's howl o'er the strangled prey.

And the hoarse refrain all day, all night,
Keeps sounding on with terrible might,
Keeps ringing its din in heedless ears—
The same old song it hath sung for years.

No rest for the waters!   Wild, bounding amain,
They leap from the mountain o'erwhelming the plain;
They laugh at all barriers, victorious and free,
Like an army they pass unrestrained to the sea.

The tempest's loud note they utter, and now
'Tis the whoop of the warrior that tramples his foe;
An anthem at morning they sound in their glee,
A requiem at eve as they pass to the sea.

MEMORIAL DAY.

[Read at the Dedication of the Soldiers' Monument in Auburn, May 30, 1882.]

Bring flowers, fresh flowers, and strew their graves,
    They fell on many a field,
Young patriots, who went forth to die,
    Their country's flag to shield.

The blooming spring, with bounteous hand,
    By every wayside spreads
Her floral wealth. Weave garlands green,
    And deck their lowly beds.

Survivors! who to arms with them
    Went forth at bugle call,—
Who with them at the front upheld
    The dear old flag thro' all:

Who bore them from the gory field
    Of battle's wild affray,—
'Tis meet we join with you and bring
    These offerings here to-day:

That fife and drum should sound again,
    And bayonets gleam once more
In honor of the illustrious dead
    Who marched with you before.

'Tis meet that from the quarry's bed,
   In life-like form should rise,
The hero of the rank and file,
   Who made such sacrifice:

That many a monumental stone
   Should bear his image high,
Conspicuous o'er the land he saved,
   Emblem of loyalty.

A grateful country lifts her voice,
   Whose children while they share
The blessings by the brave secured,
   Shall breathe perpetual prayer.

And often as the spring-time comes,
   And strews with lavish hand
Her treasures here, we'll strew these graves,
   Honored throughout the land.

DAVID BARKER.

[Died at Bangor, September 15, 1874.]

I only knew him by the strain
   He flung at random from his lyre:
Ambitious not for worldly fame,
He kept as 'twere a hidden flame
   His spark of the Promethean fire.

I never read his glowing lines
   Without a curious wish to know
How 'twas the lawyer's pen could trace,
With humorous or pathetic grace,
   Such numbers as he made to flow.

In war's dark times, when patriot hearts
   Were forced sometimes a sigh to heave;
He struck his harp to notes of cheer,
And sounded forth, high-toned and clear,
   His tribute to "The Empty Sleeve."

Some tribute to the bard is due,
   Who tribute to the soldier paid,
And helped with stirring song create,
For country and for native State,
   High hopes and courage undismayed.

How often, in his jovial moods,
　　He caught up novel themes and sung
Spontaneous rhymes !   His ready wit
Gave laughter the hysteric fit
　　And gaunt dyspepsia's nerves unstrung.

What if at times he stepped aside,
　　Discarding all restraints and rules,
And let his Muse indulge full free
A frolic for his cronies glee,
　　And called fastidious critics fools?

Not less a genuine bard was he,
　　Who stamped his impress on his lay :
So true he touched the strings at times
All hearts responded to his rhymes,
　　And yielded to their magic sway.

He joined not with the shouting crowd
　　Who in the victor cur delight :
But pour'd in quaint burlesque a strain
Of pity for the dog in pain,—
　　Despised and under in the fight :

A deed for which, methinks, howe'er
　　The shouting crowd may scoff and jeer,
He hath won friends.   With modest grace
Upon the rolls he takes his place,
　　And will be long remembered here.

IN MEMORIAM.

[Lines written in October, 1868, on the death of Hon. T. A. D. Fessenden, a member of this Bar, who died in Auburn, September 28th, of that year.]

Full soon the summer months have fled,—
    The last brief summer months for him,
Our friend and brother! Who could tell
That ere the summer's foliage fell,
    Should sound his mournful, funeral hymn?

And now the harvest days are sad,
    Too full of grief that must have way:
And autumn's tinted mantle spread
Seems as a shroud,—for he is dead,—
    Called hence, alas, ere life's noonday.

In these accustomed daily walks
    No more will his familiar face
And cordial, greeting hand be known;
And we shall miss the genial tone
    Of life in his accustomed place.

How vain are words! What sympathy
    Can soothe the sorrows now unsealed?
The heart its vigils lone must keep:
Its fitful slumbers are not sleep
    But restless yearnings unrevealed.

Speak **not of** other days and hours,
    When morning time illumed the way;
When manhood's strength and friendship's ties
Proclaim'd a man whom **we did** prize,—
    All these have quickly passed **away:**

And now the shadow and the gloom,
    The sudden dimness over all:
A blank, where that bright beacon burned,
To which the eyes of childhood turned
    With many a sweet and tender call.

Time may, perchance, assuage the **pain,**
    But cannot heal **the bleeding wound:**
Thro' months and years which are to come,
The memories of the broken home
    Will cluster tearfully around;

And fair, **young features which reveal**
    The semblance of **the father's face,**
Will speak of **him as days go on,**
And bear his impress **fixed upon**
    And fashioned to sweet childhood's grace.

THE WOOD NYMPH.

Away with your tales of the stormy, old sea!
  That music that steals o'er the thundering surge,
Is nought but the voice of a demon's wild glee,
  As it blends with the wail of the mariner's dirge.

Tell me not of your bright, coral grottoes that gleam
Far down in the depths where the daylight's glad beam
Illumines them not,—but the phosphoric glare
Of bones that untimely lie bleaching there,
Is the only, the dim, funereal light,
That fitfully shines thro' the watery night.
Say not that the mermaid all gracefully there
Is decking with sea-shells her beautiful hair,
Whose loose, flowing tresses drip wet with the spray,
Or trail o'er the waves as she urges her way;
Say not that she sports 'midst the mazes of waters,
And smiles to her sisters, the Neried daughters;
That she sleeps on the foam of the white-crested billow,
As calm as an infant reposed on its pillow;
While the sailor boy gazes entranced with delight,
Till awak'ning, she starts from her dream in affright,
And turns on him nought but a love-quelling frown,—
So he weeps when the soul of his transport hath flown.

I envy her not. The bright home of my joys
Is not where the rage of the tempest annoys;
For the wild winds of Æolus are awful to me
As they howl in their frenzy out o'er the dark sea.
I envy her not.   Ah, she knows not the bliss
Of a bower in the woodland so grateful as this,—
Where the soft skies of summer are bending above,
All mantled in beauty and radiant with love;
Where the music of waters steals soft on the ear,
And the voices of songsters say gladness is here;—
Where the twilight descends on its dim, dusky pinions
And broods like a dream o'er my fairy dominions,
Till the murmurs of evening wax fainter around,
And hush in the silence of midnight profound.

Oh, I've a sweet bank by the cool fountain's bed,
With its carpet of moss-woven daisies outspread,
And above it the wild vines, embracing each other,
Weave greenly the web of their foliage together;
Around it the wood flowers are daintily blowing,
And beside it the bright, sparkling waters are flowing,—
Here in sheltered seclusion, retired at noonday,
I recline like a queen in some fairy display,
Softly kissed by the breezes whose odorous wings
Waft the incense of bloom till the nightingale sings.
Here I hie unobserved when my pastime is over,
And laugh at the wooings of my young elfin lover,—
A rogue whom I tease till his courage is high,
Then out of his sight in a twinkle I fly.

And here, by the light of the sweet silver moon,
With the Genius of Beauty I sometimes commune;
As revealed in the light of an angel of love,
She descends thro' the blue fields of ether above,

More soft than a sylph of the twilight, to glide
O'er the realms where the graces of Nature preside.
Fair Hebe with cheeks of the rose is my guest,
With the glory of childhood and innocence blest;
And the blue-eyed Endymion, who, slumbering at night,
Made the heart of Diana throb wild with delight.
They come,—not creations of fable and dream,
But living realities, fair as they seem:
I welcome their coming and bid them recline
On my green, mossy bank 'neath the clambering vine,
While stars thro' the foliage peep down from on high,
And the belted Orion flames bright in the sky.

But not to the woodlands alone am I bound:
The green, spreading meadows and streamlets around,
The lawns and the uplands, the glens and the groves,
Are scenes where my spirit exultingly roves.
I am forth at the dawn ere the twilight doth pale,—
When the blushing Aurora her charms doth unveil,
And the gates of the morning swing open, and day
With its chariot of sunbeams proceeds on its way.
At noontide I glide to the skirt of the wood;
A moment I stand where the husbandman stood,
And I note all his movements, tho' never does he
Catch a glimpse, in his wandering vision, of me.
I glance at the cottager's little ones at play
Seen far thro' the trees in the distance away,
And I smile at their frolics as jocund and light
As the gambols of fairies at midsummer night.
I trace to its source the meandering rill;
I pause on the brow of the neighboring hill,
And watch till the day god doth close his career,
And his banners of crimson and gold disappear.

The world hath a sphere close by dwellings of men,
Which none but the spirits immortal can ken,—
A fairy bright realm, widely peopled, which seems
To the senses of mortals a net-work of dreams.
In that region we dwell, and are never revealed
Save to fancy's bright eye with its vision unsealed:
There we troop with the dryads and throng at the shrine
Of Nature, and worship our goddess divine.

'Tis meet for us, then, at the stillness of eve
A hymn to her praises in concert to weave;
As we sit all along where the clear waters lave,
And the fringe of the willows droops over the wave.
    'Tis meet for us always, by moonlight and grove,
To swell on the soft winds our anthems of glee,—
    Tho' a mystery to mortals, we live and we move
Like the spirits of air unfettered and free.

SUMMER AND SUNSET.

Alone amidst the hills !
Here have I wandered by the joyous rills,
And caught the music sweet
Of unseen harps which charm this lone retreat ;
Here have I plucked the flower
That blooms uncultured in its natural bower,
And snuffed the odors rare
That load with fragrance all the mountain air.
I've rested by the pool,
Where on my forehead breathed the west wind cool ;
And by its margin green,
Almost the sporting fairies have I seen,
Plying their mazy dance
With nods and becks and laughing eyes askance.

Then up the woodland reach
My steps I've turned, beyond the groves of beech,
Beyond the maple glades,
That weave a twilight of their emerald shades,
And pausing on the brow
Of yonder highland, viewed the scene below ;
Viewed thence the sleeping lake,
Without a ripple save the barge's wake,
To mar its gentle rest,
Or fret the welkin pictured on its breast ;
Viewed thence the giant wood,
A remnant of the old primeval brood,

Whose oaks of hoary age,
Stand yet unscathed, despite the winter's rage;
Beheld the farmer's pride
Of waving grain fields on the green hill-side,
And gardens in their bloom,
And orchards bending with the pear and plum;
And seen the hamlet, too,
Lapped in the valley where the stream winds thro',
But heard not thence the hum
Of busy life in echoing murmurs come:
Hushed in the distant scene
It lay, with steeple in the sunlight sheen,
With church-yard just in sight,
Whose marble grave-stones gleamed all snowy white;
With many a cottage lost
In foliage thickening like the forest host;
With monarch elms on high,
Stretching their green arms thro' the azure sky,
Wide over peaceful homes,
Across whose thresholds no intruder comes.

And now the setting sun,
Throned in the west, the goal of evening won,
Seemed pausing to behold
The world illumined by his beams of gold.
A *cortége* of bright clouds
Unfurled about his chariot course in crowds,
Assumed fantastic shapes,
And flung the drapery of their crimson capes
Around each changing form,
That glanced in light and waved its victor palm.
Along the horizon's verge,
I saw afar their glittering hosts emerge,

With panoply and plume,
And banners woven in the solar loom,
    And blazonry of gems,
That flashed in brilliance from their burnished helms.
    In gleaming cohorts now
Thro' shifting march, in mystic maze, they go;
    And ever as they change,
Throughout the bright fields of their boundless range,
    Exulting arms they wave,
And lift their banners buoyant as the brave,
    In homage to that orb,
Whose beams of life rejoicing worlds absorb.

    But as the pageant fades,
They roll their fleece-cloaks in the gathering shades,
    Undo their feathery wreaths,
And pluck the finery from their gilded sheaths;
    Folding them slow away,
For now the twilight waits not on the day,
    But o'er the hills descends,
And into dimness all their beauty blends.

POESY.

Spirit of Nature, thou,
Who hast thy dwelling here,
Amidst these walks of men,
Accessible to all!
Whose shrine is where the dark woods frown
When swathed in winter's gloom,
Not less than midst the gorgeous haunts
Of summer!

Spirit of Nature, thou,
Mysterious power unseen,
Unseen yet visible
In myriad wondrous works;
In every life, in every change revealed;
As marvelous in the gathering shades
Of each returning even,
As in the radiant glories numberless,
Which throng the night sky or unfold at morn!

Spirit, supreme o'er all,
Intelligent and good!
Whose power alone it is
To move the dull heart from its lethargy,
And strike its chords in unison
With all the quiring harps of nature,—
How shall we learn of thee,
How learn and learning live!

Not of ourselves is 't given
To see the wondrous whole:
Not of ourselves to pierce

The mystic veil impenetrable,
Which, like a cloud before the orient dawn,
　　Hides from our finite view,
The pure, bright essence of the Infinite.

　Yet Deity which is in all,
　　Above, around, beneath ;
　　Which holds and tempers all,—
Hath so diffused its universal being,
　So touched with life created things,
　　That e'en the frailest forms
　　Of matter organized,
　Speak of the unseen Presence :
　　While inert nature hath
A yet more marvelous language, argument
　O'erriding dreams of chance,
And eloquence and anthemed harmonies,—
　Perpetual life song of a world,
　Which, aye, thro' all the details of
　Its vast and varied mechanism,
　　Reveals the spirit impulse.

　Creation's marvelous book,
'Tho' oped to all, is by how few explored !
Its plainest lessons learned how meagerly !
Its deeper meaning, the mysterious lore
　Wherewith each glowing page is set,
　　How seldom fathomed !

　Earth, ocean, air, and sky,
　　Illustrious brotherhood !
And you, ye ever-wandering orbs,
Whose march is thro' the vague immensity ;
　Whose far-off music steals
　At times on gifted ears,

And wakes within the human soul,
Those glowing ecstasies that spring
Not from an earthly measure!

Ye lakes and valleys wild,
That slumber midst the forest hills
In solitary loveliness,
And never feel the boisterous breath of winter!
How beautiful are ye! From out
Your hushed retreats mysterious chimes I hear;
And from your coverts echo-thronged,
Come moving melodies,
Attuned by airy sprites that touch,
When twilight broods around,
The harp strings of the wilderness.

And you, ye mouutains old,
Stupendous, awful, grand!
Piled to the heavens, yet unbowed beneath
The burden of your native majesty:
Upon whose naked, hoary heads
The desolating years have shed their snows,
Their icy snows of age;
And midst whose dreary loneliness,
Supremely throned, bald monarch of the waste,
Gray solitude hath held his reign
In unmolested grandeur from the first:—
What marvelous power have ye
To stir the musing soul!

And you, ye rocks, and cliffs, and crags,
Tumultuous-born, upheaved from earth,
And frowning o'er the sea:
Against whose iron battlements
The warring winds have waged

Relentless strife, and the rude tempest raised
  His Titan arm in vain :
 How wonderful are ye ! Not mute
And motionless, but living monitors,
  Ye stand ; and, voiceful still with praise,
  Instinct with inspiration,
  Eloquent with breathing harmonies,
Ye speak unto the poet's soul,—that soul
   Which owns nature its mother,
   Kindles at her voice and leaps
   Exulting to her arms, to catch
The faintest accents of her whispered lore,—
  Ye speak unto the poet's soul,
Stirring its inmost fountains with a sense
   Of all the beautiful and grand ;
  Till with life's bounding pulse elate,
  It bursts into its native utterance
   And pours itself in song.

   Genius of Poesy, then,
  Whose essence doth pervade
All things that are,—who speakest from the stars,
  That nightly sentinel the sky :
   Whose voice is in the sea ;
 And from the lakes and valleys comes,
 And from the sylvan shades remote,
   Where wild birds make their homes ;
Who soundest forth from solitary woods,
From rocks and mountains and the lonely shore,
  Harmonious notes of minstrelsy,
   That reach the secret ear ;—
   The soul that yearns for thee,
  Need never ask where thou dost dwell,
   Nor how with bended knee
   To supplicate thine aid.

Nature and thou are one:
The legends of old classic lore,
Which made Parnassus' misty height
Home of the Muses nine;
Or with the tuneful choir
Peopled the groves of Helicon,
And told of fountains whose inspiring drafts
Could wake to life the old, heroic strains,
Or prompt such glowing lays
As burning Sappho sung,—
Tho' beautiful, were vain:
For not the Grecian mountains old,
Nor all the sacred groves and founts
Of that immortal land,
Could compass thy domain :—
The universe was thine.

Upon yon fleecy clouds
That sweep the sky, thy chariot moves serene:
Thou 't heard in every passing breeze,
E'en in the zephyr's sigh:
Seen always 'midst the joyous hills,
And found by every stream,
That courses 'neath the pendent boughs
Of summer.

The soul that yearns for thee,
Has but to hold its silent intercourse
Apart in Nature's temple,
To gain the wished-for boon.
The eye is there unsealed;
Slumber's lethargic spell is broken,
And the glad heart, to truer life awakened,
Drinks in the thrilling symphonies
Of myriad lyres unseen,
All touched to one accordant minstrelsy,
E'en by the Master hand.

THE PEARL OF MARANOCOOK.

[It is within the remembrance of many persons now living that remnants of the aboriginal tribes who formerly peopled New England, were accustomed to visit, from time to time, certain localities in this State, usually selecting for their encampment some retired and secluded spot on the borders of our romantic lakes, and oftentimes remaining for months, pursuing their original avocations and preserving to a large extent their primitive modes of life. The interest and curiosity awakened among the younger portion of the community, in the days of our boyhood, by the advent of such visitors to the shores, or neighboring highlands, of Lake Maranocook are vividly retained in memory. And although as a rule the specimens of the race seen there on such occasions were not the best modeled types of humanity, yet there were occasional exceptions, which, for native grace and beauty, might challenge the admiration of our best schools of taste and refinement. The picture attempted to be drawn in this poem, though for the most part imaginary, had its first suggestion in impressions received on a boyish excursion to the Indian encampment near that now well-known and picturesque sheet of water, which recent enterprise has made so attractive and christened with its Indian name, Maranocook.]

Tell me the secret of that power,
Beauty that rules the wide world o'er?
Is it of teeming-fancy bred,
Whim of the heart or of the head?
Say how developed, how combined ;
Whence is its magic touch refined
That holds the eye and steals the heart
As if by talismanic art?
No studied skill unfolds the flower,—
Pray, tell me whence is Beauty's power !

What tho' a daughter of the wood,
Born of the twilight dusky-hued,—
Without the azure-tinted eye
With which the light-haired blonde may vie ;

11

Disclosing on her cheek the tawn
Whereof the wild deer's young are born,
Save softened to that paler tinge
With which the curtained eve doth fringe
The daylight when the setting sun
Down o'er the western hill hath gone!

I saw her by the margin stand
Of her own native lake,—a strand
Where yet the pale-faced pioneer
Had entered not on his career,
But all of natural mould was free
And wildly beautiful as she.
Was it the dreamy light and shade
Of romance to my eye portrayed?
Some fickle, fairy sprite that roved
The earth or air, my fancy moved?
Some gypsy maid who wrought a spell
Of glamour potent to compel
Spontaneous homage, ere a word
Or accent from the tongue were heard?

Methought,—what wonder?—as I viewed
Her presence by the skirting wood,
That never yet did chisel trace
A figure of symmetric grace
Where rounded arm and neck and waist
Were fashioned to a purer taste:
That never yet did form combine
In earthly mould so much divine.
Rather that one of earth she seemed
Some bright ideal I had dreamed
When reading of the graces given
To houries in the Moslem heaven.

But talk not of the sculptor's art,
Nor yet of dreams.   Dreams but impart
False coloring to fictitious gems,
Which life's more earnest sense condemns.
Talk rather of the young gazelle
Within its own wild mountain dell ;
Talk of the birds on joyous wing,
That make the forest echoes ring ;
Name all the varied beauties seen
Where nature undisturbed hath been,
But leave to grace some other theme
The Parian stone and poet's dream.

Such was the type of life displayed
Within the dark-eyed Indian maid,
As on the lake's romantic shore
Her wealth of simple grace she bore,—
A grace which nature scarcely gave
The full-blown lily on the wave.
Tall and erect, she stood serene,
Slender of form, yet in her mien
Revealing that true, natural charm,
That cast of feature, neck, and arm,
Which did the eye of fancy fill
And almost shamed the artist's skill.
She stood as stands young forest tree,
Most comely on its native lea,—
Around whose stock and branches twine
The tendrils of the trailing vine
In many a graceful curve and turn,
As dainty as the maiden-fern.
Like some coy daughter of the morn,
Walking the hill-side slopes at dawn,
And child-like pausing oft to greet,
The views where woods and waters meet ;

Turning unveiled her frequent gaze
Full to the morn's unclouded blaze,—
She moved,—herself a morning beam,
As joyous as the mountain stream:
A peerless picture painted there
Of radiant life, surpassing fair.

No fairer landscape greets the sight:
No lovelier lake with waters bright
Mirrors the wide, surrounding scene
Of wooded hills and meadows green,
Blending all charms to please the eye.
None paints with deeper blue the sky,
Or turns more graceful to the view
The ripple of the light canoe.
What wonder that the maiden there
Caught many a charm from scene so fair,
And many a charm returned as she
The mountain pathway threaded free,
Her locks of ebon, loose, undone,
Her dark eye flashing to the sun,
Her dusky face reflecting bright
The glowing soul's untaught delight?
Methought the radiance of her smile
Enough to charm the forest aisle,
Investing lake and wood and vale
With romance like Arabian tale.

What if the bright sun's fervid glance
O'er her young bosom's free expanse.
O'er beaded neck and hoodless brow,
Had poured its full, its ardent glow,
And tinged to deeper dusk the hue
Which first her virgin features knew?

Not less the Indian maiden seemed
To wear each grace, each charm redeemed.
Ye might have thought a gem so fair
Was strangely set to glisten there.
Have deemed her an exotic here,
A creature of some brighter sphere,
Nurtured in some far, tropic isle
Where summer skies incessant smile
And 'neath the palms and orange boughs
Her wealth of beauty Nature shows.

Strange,—that the forest depths should be
Meet home for her so young and free;
That pathways devious, which but led
Where fleet the Indian hunter sped,
Or where the young-eyed, playful fawn
Springs lightly forth to greet the dawn,
Should hold in their retired retreats
A bloom which Nature rare repeats!
How was it that the forest wild
Won to itself so fair a child?
What magic had the woodland glens
Whose deeper haunts the red man kens,
What magic the wild lakes and streams
Beside whose waves the camp fire gleams,
To tempt Dame Nature's cunning skill
Her daintiest work there to fulfill?

Ah, if the light of beauty's eye
Is brilliant where gay banners fly,
And pageantry of pomp and power
Illustrious rules the golden hour,—

And if the dreamy sylphs of air
That flaunt the halls of splendor where
Exulting mirth and music sweet
Lead on the maze of twinkling feet,
And lustrous eyes responsive glance,
And joy whirls giddy in the dance,—
Are beauteous to the gay world's gaze
And first receive its meed of praise;
Yet far removed from scenes like these,
Whose burnished wealth and splendor please,
Dwell types of beauty meet to claim
A record on the lists of fame.

Not in the heart or in the head
Is beauty's *beau ideal* bred:
The perfect art which bears the palm
For native grace and native charm,
And readiest homage doth command,
Is found alone in Nature's hand.

MY VOLUME OF BURNS.

A POEM FOR THE ANNIVERSARY OF THE POETS' BIRTH-DAY.

—

Sometimes at close of hard day's work,
Beset with cares I cannot shirk,
Depressed, bewildered, giving vent
To bootless spleen and discontent;

I wander home unsettled quite,—
A curtain like the murky night
Hangs o'er my soul, and yet I know
My sky should not be clouded so.

A voice within me whispers then,
Lift up thy heart like other men,
And let the home light's cosy cheer
Shine in.   What boots depression here?

I share the clean-spread, evening board,
For me the genial cup is poured,
I smile—aha. that genial cup
Hath waked my better nature up.

O blest nepenthe!   Light within,
A rainbow where the cloud hath been!
Lo, I have friends,—my life-blood starts
Responsive to their throbbing hearts.

Rare friends whose love and sympathy
Flowed out for dear humanity;
Living tho' dead,—ay, standing there,
Companions by my evening chair.

Old Spenser, Moore, Scott, Milton, Keats,
Shakespeare, whose verse the world repeats,—
I prize them all; but my heart turns
Most lovingly to Robert Burns,

Whose pleasant face smiles from the shelf
On that rare volume, all himself;
Rich treasury of the heart's own songs.
Which to the world at large belongs.

Not Scotland's heathery banks and braes
Could circumscribe her poet's lays;
Nor can her sons exclusive claim
The heritage of his great name.

His magic strains have found their way
Where'er the Muse hath power to sway,
And moved with sympathetic glee
The great heart of humanity.

I ope and read that charming lay,
Night of the cotter's Saturday;
And hear the good man's prayer ascend
To Him, Protector, Father, Friend.

I share the poet's tender love
For Mary's soul in Heaven above;
And almost feel his grief my own,
So touchingly his heart makes moan.

I see the modest, crimson flower
That met him in the " evil hour,"
Crushed by the plowshare, and I feel
The beauty of his sweet appeal.

And now before my very eyes
The panic-stricken mousie hies,
As, crash, into his " wee bit " home
The coulter brings relentless doom.

If I would laugh, why, then, instanter,
I turn to jolly Tam O'Shanter,
The brick, who all the sage advices
Of a good wife derides, despises ;

And while the hapless woman worries
Off on a bender straight he hurries,
And sprees it late, till tempests lower
And brimstone scents the midnight hour

I see him homeward draw the rein
On frightened Mag, with anxious strain,
Giving full many a lively jerk
As now he nears the haunted kirk,

Where, by the lightning's sudden glance
Revealed, the witches' jig and dance ;
Led on by Nan, the cutty sark,
Thro' reels, mysterious, strange, and dark.

I see him pause to spy the fun,
I hear his lusty shout, " weel done ! "
When, presto ! it is dark as soot,—
And out they rush in swift pursuit.

The bold in wassail, where is now
The pluck he ne'er would disavow?
They'll have him by the lightning's gleam,
Ere he can pass the running stream.

Right brisk the race for life begins ;
Slim chance for Tam, whose many sins
Weigh hard on him and Maggie, **too,**
Pursued by such a hellish crew.

They clutch at Tam who dodges, pale,
They grab for Maggie's switching tail,
They scatter brimstone,—Nan, the hag,
A special vengeance has for Mag.

O for the key-stone o' the bridge !
Three leaps and Mag will clear the ridge
And pass triumphant o'er the water,
And save a hapless soul from slaughter.

But hold your senses ! Who can **tell**
What chances in **a moment dwell,**
Or why when pluck bids fair to win,
Old Nick should **ofttimes claw us in ?**

Whisk o'er the key-stone ! **Hey !** But, lo,
One swoop and the remorseless foe,
Takes off with grappling claw and nail,
All that could switch o' Maggie's tail ;

And with the trophy off they skelp,—
Tam cursing loud both hag and whelp,
And moaning Maggie's untoward fate,
Crossing the stream a moment late.

Ah, many moments late for **Tam !**
The wife's advice was not a **sham.**
Foul luck betides his evil ways,
He'll smell o' brimstone all his days ;

While Maggie, in dismembered plight,
A melancholy, shocking sight,
Shall never more when fiends assail,
Shake at the foe a wrathful tail.

I close the volume—but mine ear
Is ringing with an accent clear,
And to my heart full oft returns
Thy glowing line,—sweet Robert Burns.

And whilst the days and years go on,
Tho' much be lost and little won,
I'll thank thee for the hours made bright
With songs which thou hast sung aright;

For melody, and wit, and glee,
The charm of thy rare minstrelsy;
And tender words of love and cheer,
Which human hearts delight to hear.

I'll thank thee for thy bonnie gems,
Sweet flowerets on their native stems,
Sprung from the soil, and therefore prized,—
Life's tears and smiles immortalized.

Lays which thy visioned Coila made
Thy special care, when soft she laid
Her hand upon thy forehead fair,
And gently bound the holly there;

Charging thou ne'er should turn aside
From these the pathways thou hadst tried,
Foreshadowing thine the brilliant fame
That keeps a gifted poet's name.

YESTER-NIGHT.

[The mysterious connection between mind and matter is a problem no nearer solution now than before its investigation was first attempted by meta-physicians. We may trace the influences of man's mental and physical organizations upon each other, and find abundant evidence of the intimate relations which exist between the two, and of the wonderful sensitiveness with which, under certain circumstances, the one receives impressions from the other: but how these effects are produced must always remain an inquiry which our limited intelligence cannot answer.

The following poem owes its original conception, in part, to a personal experience. It is not altogether a fiction in the sense in which ordinary work of the imagination is a fiction. But while it finds no counterpart in reality, it is nevertheless a reflection of those strange associations which sometimes pass through the mind, in the crises of acute diseases, when the physical organs are disturbed and fail to perform their normal functions, and the governing powers of consciousness and volition lose control. Something kindred to this may, at times, have fallen within the experience of many individuals. Such vagaries are not, however, an inviting subject for poetical composition, nor even an attractive theme to contemplate. They are apt to assume too much the character of a phantasm, and like the visions of the opium eater, rule the mind with relentless energy, administering quite as frequently to painful as pleasurable emotions. The poem was written many years ago and is, perhaps, ill-adapted to this or any other publication. It is, nevertheless, among the papers, which fact must explain the reason for its appearance here.]

Yester-night, methought, the moonlight
   Gave a strange, unnatural glow
To the tombstones in the church-yard
   And the grave mounds white with snow.

And a presence from the dimness
   Met me hurriedly and said :
" Wanderer in the cold, gray midnight,
   Go not near the sleeping dead."

Then from many voices came there
   Suddenly a sound of wail,
And the forms of some familiar
   Crossed my pathway, ashy pale.

Oh, methought, how changed their features!
    Visages so overcast,
And their strange transfiguration,
    Made me shudder as they passed.

One there was who as she hastened
    Turned a passing glance on me,
Waved a shadowy hand, and straightway
    Vanished into mystery.

Disappointment, anxious longing,
    Doubt and fear my soul oppressed ;
And there came a sense of trouble
    And a burden of unrest.

But I strove to quell the anguish,
    And the fear to lay aside ;—
Hoping still some blessed unction
    Of relief would soon betide.

For the precious balm of healing
    Is a blessing unalloyed
To the brain oppressed, bewildered,
    Tortured by the fierce typhoid ;

And the gentle power of slumber,
    Sent from heaven to soothe our woes,
O'er the waters of our trouble
    Poureth oil of sweet repose.

Here with something of composure
    I regained, methought, at length
My self-possession,—yet was wakeful,
    Weary, faint, and lacking strength.

Still my heart yearned for deliverance
    From that demon whose control
Cast such shadow o'er my vision,
    Laid such burden on my soul.

Long I watched intently listening,
    Till the dim, uncertain light
Waned, methought, and all was shrouded
    In the mystery of the night.

Presently the plaintive murmurs
    Of a distant, tolling bell
Rose upon the night air, sounding
    Sad as maiden's funeral knell.

Then a strain of low, sweet music
    Came and died upon mine ear:—
Nothing else disturbed the stillness,
    Not a living wight was near.

I was marveling much and doubtful
    What the sequel yet might be,
Pondering many a vague conjecture
    What mine eyes were next to see ;

When an ever-wakeful night bird
    Shrieked, methought, from out a wood,
And the ominous cry did startle
    E'en the night-born solitude.

" Heavens ! " I cried, " What fearful meaning
    Hath this wild bird's dismal scream,
Breaking thus upon the midnight
    Like the nightmare in a dream?

" Cometh doom and retribution,
    Heralded at such an hour
By this hoarse and hideous outcry,
    Signal of an evil power?"

Not a voice my query answered:
    All again was hushed and still;
But a fearful apprehension,
    As of some foreboded ill,

Came with feverish tremblings o'er me,
    And the cold sweat on my brow
Gathered like the frosts of winter,
    When the sun sets cold and low.

Night at length did wane, and morning
    Walked the hill-tops of the east:
But the pale moon still kept watching,
    Sank not with the stars to rest.

As the day toiled slowly upward,
    All its glories seemed to fade:
Lurid sunlight, pallid moonlight,
    But a dismal twilight made.

Change was on the face of nature;
    And the far hills' distant range,
And more near the haunts familiar
    Wore an aspect deathly strange.

Men were forth in streets and by-ways
    Terror-stricken and dismayed,
Fearful even of each other,
    Groping lonely and afraid.

One, an old man, faint and weary,
  By a little child led on,
Dropped, as of a sudden palsy,
  Died and left the child alone.

All alone, bereaved, bewildered,
  None to speak to, none to hear,—
"O, thou pitying God!" I faltered,
  "Stretch thine arm of mercy near."

Then a mother hurrying frantic,
  With her infant in her arms,
Called aloud on heaven to shield her
  From unknown and nameless harms.

He, the father, on whose strong arm,
  Trustful she was wont to lean,
Lurked afar, in cold estrangement,
  Wore a wild, unearthly mien.

Sweet hope and trust and sympathy,
  Love that bids the tear to start,
No token gave. No kindly impulse
  Spake within the human heart.

Even the beasts of earth and wild birds
  Caught the panic fright full soon;
From kenneled sleep awoke the watch-dog
  And behowled the spectral moon.

Dismal wails and piercing outcries
  Heard I then ring through the air,
As if frenzied fiends were scourging
  All the victims of despair.

Holy Heaven! I scarce could murmur
 E'en the semblance of a prayer,—
Heaven, methought, had given us over
 Without warning to prepare.

In that wild and strange confusion,
 In the darkness gathering there,
Listening, fearful, heard I uttered
 Loud the startling word: Prepare!

Thrice a voice above the tumult,
 Like the midnight thunder's boom,
Gave, methought, the dreadful summons,
 Sounded forth the word of doom.

Earth and ocean's deep foundations,
 Seemed it then, were giving way;
Yawned a chasm like an earthquake's
 And the mountains were its prey.

And the rush of mighty waters
 Came with overwhelming power,—
Ruin, waste, and desolation,
 Night and darkness had their hour.

Blind and palsied by the horrors
 Of that fearful scene I stood,
Dazed, senseless,—on some scant foot-hold
 Reached not by the rolling flood:

On some fragment of an island,
 Where, in seething malstrom whirled,
Wide around were dashed the remnants
 Of a lost and shipwrecked world.

12

Passed the crisis : soon subsided
　　The wild tumult, and no more
Rang the bootless cries of anguish.
　　Mingled with the tempest's roar.

But the silence that succeeded
　　Brought no rest unto my soul.—
O'er my couch the fever demon
　　Still asserted his control.

Still with grasp of iron held me,
　　Yielding scarce a respite now
From the visions which had torn me.
　　Crushed me with their fearful show.

Here the low voice of the watcher
　　Sought to soothe my sense of fear,
And a soft hand on my forehead
　　Wiped the cold drops standing there :

And my incoherent fancies
　　Ceased their dismal march awhile,
And the pitying heart beside me
　　With a dear hope dared to smile.

Calmer grew my troubled spirit,
　　And a spell of natural sleep
Came and sealed awhile my senses,
　　And its mastery seemed to keep

In check th' oppressed brain's tendency
　　To drift into that shoreless sea,—
Passing once whose gloomy confines,
　　All is doubt and mystery.

When from that sweet space of slumber
    I awakened, lo! the sun.
Beaming with his morning splendor,
    Had a better day begun.

And my heart drank in the gladness
    Of the blessed morning light,
Gleaming on the crystal hill-tops,
    And the snowy landscape bright.

I had passed from out that dimness ;
    But those shadows on my soul
Traced a tablet, and the vision
    Haunts me spite all self-control.

UNCLE JABE.

pp. 192, 193.

CENTENNIAL POEM.

[Read at Winthrop, Me., May 20, 1871, on the occasion of the celebration of the one hundredth anniversary of the incorporation and organization of the town.]

One hundred years ago!   Shall I presume
To wander backward through a century's gloom,
With lyre unstrung, unskilled to gain renown,
And sing the birthday of this good old town?
Shall I essay, with laboring verse, to tell
Historic tales of what our sires befell
In those old days, when Pond Town was a wild
Where men like hermits lived, nor woman smiled;
Those old, colonial days, when George the Third
Ruled all the land with his puissant sword,
And sought to force oppression's galling yoke
On subjects loyal, till their souls awoke
With sense of wrongs too grievous to be borne,
And spurned the sceptered monarch on his throne?

Is such a theme the theme for me to choose;
And will the Muses my dull heart infuse
With life and fire, so I may strike some chord
That shall a fitting harmony afford;
So I may wake some echo of a strain,
Though brief and faint, perchance not all in vain;
Nor feel o'erwhelmed lest my unfinished task
Should need indulgence more than I can ask?
Kind friends, forgive, and stray with me along,
Nor turn at this, the prelude of the song.

One hundred years ago, this very day,
The first town-meeting (so the records say)
Was held at an innholder's house, which means
Not what some college boys, with roguish spleens,
Might half surmise, a place where all within
Are held by one without who holds them in ;
But simply that the meeting was convened
At an old tavern stand wherein was weaned
The infant town, then christened, named anew,
And clothed with corporate powers with much ado.
On that great day,—*anno urbis conditæ*,—
No doubt the landlord did his bounden duty,
And furnished freely all the needful aid,
To have that corner-stone most fitly laid.
Perhaps a bumper crowned the festive board,
Perhaps with merriment the table roared ;
For in those times the keeper of an inn
Most always kept a little " smile " within.
No doubt the yoeman did good service, too,
And put the thing magnificently through :
Chose selectmen and constable and clerk,
And all officials, setting them at work
With busy hands, to make the new-made town
A little jewel in King George's crown ;
For in his Majesty's ungracious name,
The warrant issued, and the people came.

Thus organized and fairly under way,
Our little ship of State set sail that day
With much of pride and more of future hope,
To brave the storms and with the billows cope.
One plucky man, who from New Ipswich came
Some years before,—John Chandler was his name,—
Held by conditional grant, as it would seem,
Hundreds of acres near the old mill stream,

And made his title good by building mills.
This led to opening roads amongst the hills.
Giving the outside settlers chance to come
And cart their loads of meal and lumber home.
And there were other names worthy of note,
Conspicuous, mighty, in those times remote.
Emblazoned on the records, sending down
Leaven enough to leaven half the town :
Foster, Fairbanks, Stevens, Pullen and Howe,
Whiting, Brainard, Stanley, and Bishop, too :
Cognomens which in poetry work in
Most musical,—as pretty as a pin.
I cannot mention all—suffice to say
They were illustrious in that ancient day,
And for the town did much,—did more, say some,
Than Romulus and Remus did for Rome.

Other town-meetings followed at the inn ;
In which the freeholders did now begin
To act on matters, some of grave import,
Discussed and passed as in the general court.
Grave-yards were purchased, and highways improved ;
Bridges were built, and obstacles removed,
Until the river towns beyond the streams
Could now be reached by teamsters with their teams.
Groceries were started, and West India goods
Toiled slowly in through miles of dreary woods,
The heavy wagon creaking 'neath its load,
The jaded oxen careless of the goad,
The weary teamster stopping now and then
To quench his thirst, then shout " gee up," again.
Improvements still advanced, the woods gave way
To waving grain-fields and the reaper's sway ;
And the broad acres, newly-cleared and burned,
Abundant harvests for the toil returned.

They voted money,—pounds and shillings, pence,
In those old days to pay the town's expense ;
They levied taxes on the estates and polls,
Which were collected like the miller's tolls :
They ordered men into the box by three's,
To serve as jurors in the Common Pleas ;
They favored learning and established schools,
Warned out of town all stragglers, idlers, fools.
Expurgating the trash like tares from wheat,
Reserving only so much as was meet
For this good town, whose honored name should be
A synonym for good society.
Religion, too, found early footing here ;
Preaching was hired eight Sabbaths in a year,
And twenty pounds were raised to pay the bills
Ere yet a meeting-house stood on its sills.
And they were careful, too, what men they hired
To preach the gospel from the word inspired,
And sometimes voted that they only would
Hire those whose moral character was good.

The history of the town hath once been writ ;
Much there that's told of course we here omit ;
Yet one or two good things therein set forth
A moment's rhyme we think are richly worth,—
For instance this, illustrative of manners
When men wore homespun, women used bandannas.

A Mr. F. once pillioned his old horse
And started off ('twas then a thing of course)
And asked a visit from a Mrs. Wood.
Quoth she : " I'd go 'n a moment if I could,
But I'm a kneading bread which I must bake."
" If that is all," quoth Mr. F., " I'll make
The pathway clear. Just take your kneading-trough
And jump upon my nag and we'll be off."

No sooner said than done. Both on the beast
With trough and bread, a funny jag at least,
Went trotting back to house of Mr. F.,
Where they arrived but little out of breath.
He built a fire, she baked her batch of bread,
She spent the day, at night went home to bed
Same style,—riding as gaily on the pillion
As modern girls would dance a brisk cotillion.

A certain fiddler, most presumptuous grown,
Once pitched his tent without permit, in town.
The good folks rallied, but ne'er raised a rout:
In a most legal way they warned him out.
The constable, whose christian name was Squier
And surname Bishop, loosed, 'tis said, his ire
And in a rage e'en warned him off God's earth.
Whereat the fiddler trembled at his wrath,
And asking where to go, was answered plain:
" Why go, you stupid fool, go out to Wayne."

One most consummate nuisance in those days
Was Dr. Gardiner's dam, with no fish ways,
Down at the mouth of Cobb'see Conte stream,—
A source of trouble which got up great steam:
For the old settlers they were fond of fish,
And half subsisted on that brain-food dish:
But Dr. Gardiner's dam built tight and high
Embargoed all the fish from passing by,
Spoiling the up-stream fishermen's delights,
Infringing, too, the fishes' vested rights,
Wronging both men and fish,—a twofold grief
Which called for some prompt action for relief.
What should be done? Ah, Dr. G., take heed.
You'll catch it now for your unfriendly deed!

They called a new town-meeting and let off
At first a protest, like a gentle cough
Before a sneeze, choosing a board of three
To coax a fish way out of Doctor G.
Coaxing was vain : The Doctor, he said no ;
No fish around or through his dam should go.
Whereat the settlers fired a louder gun,
Remonstrating and threatening both in one.
Here was a *casus belli*, cause of war
More palpable than Greek and Trojan saw.
They did not fight to right this double wrong
But fired full many a protest loud and strong,
And boldly voted,—choosing every year
A fresh committee to present more clear
Their grievances against that stubborn dam.
Which locked the stream where once good fishes swam.
Alack a day ! Not ten, long, voting years,
With double-shotted protests barbed like spears,
Availed them aught. That dam it would not down ;
So finally,—they let the thing alone.

But, hark ! There is a tumult in the land,
And a more serious conflict now at hand,
A conflict not of merely local strife,
But one in which a people strike for life.
England, harsh mother, from her sea-girt isle,
Bloated with wealth of many lands the spoil,
Drunken with power—proud mistress of the sea,
Lays heavy tribute by her stern decree
On all the provinces throughout the land ;
Their voice in council hushed by her command,
Their sacred, chartered rights all cloven down,
Their ministers spurned even from the throne,
The people, helpless, crying for redress,
The monarch laughing at their vain distress.

Ah, there were murmurings gathering wide and far,
And stern resolves for justice, else for war.
A voice from old Virginia loyal then,
Electrified the hearts of living men
With words of fire, till flew on every breath
The clarion war-cry : " Liberty or death ! "

And where was Winthrop on that trying day?
Did she not arm in earnest for the fray?
Ay, this old township heard the trumpet call
And sent her sons to conquer or to fall.
Those were the times that tried men's souls.   Alas !
Should her young sons the dread ordeal pass,
And come again to these their hill-side homes
To spend their days and find their burial tombs?
Heaven only knew what was in store for them.
Who speeds the right will sure the wrong condemn !
Prompt at their country's call a score went forth
To the provincial army of the North
Then mustering at old Cambridge, marshaling
To meet the red-coat squadrons of the King.
The blood that flowed from many a mortal wound
At Lexington lay fresh upon the ground,
And the raw infantry were on the drill
For their grand charge at glorious Bunker Hill.
But this is history,—and I need not tell
A tale which every school-boy knows full well.
Only the part this patriotic town
Took in the contest should be written down,
And honorable mention made of those
Who joined the ranks against the country's foes.
But few returned to these new homes to dwell :
Some died of hardship,—some in battle fell,
And some who privateered came back from sea
To share the blessings of a country free.

We must not loiter longer on the way
To tell what happened in the olden day.
Let us unfurl our light sails to the breeze,
And like a good ship o'er the laughing seas,
Glide onward through the lapse of rolling years.
A wayward pilot is the Muse, who steers
Sometimes a devious course,—too prone to dash
The craft on breakers with a fearful crash,
Making appalling shipwreck.   Let us try
And pass the dangerous breakers safely by,
Bringing our good ship to the offing now
Of later days,—a port which we do know.
Lo, here we come with all our canvas free !
The gleaming beacons on the strand we see,
The old, familiar shores, the rocks, the hills.
The emerald fields, sweet lakes and streams and rills,—
A thousand scenes in memory treasured well,
Crowd into view with many a tale to tell.

Dear native town !   May I not bring to thee
A passing tribute, slight howe'er it be,
Some little word, a token fondly laid
Upon the altar where our childhood played ;
And where a musing fancy loved to roam,
Enraptured with the beautiful at home?
May I not pause one moment to renew
The dear delights which laughing boyhood knew,
Here where the hills hold in their sweet embrace
So many a lakelet, touched with native grace ;
Here where the woods in spring-time were so green,
And all the landscape seemed a fairy scene ;
Here where we wandered, truants from the school,
And penance paid for many a broken rule,—
Loving the freedom of the woodlands more
Than all the tasks the teacher had in store,

And willing martyrs to the rod, if we
Could thus atone for this our truant glee?
Was it the weakness of a boyish heart
To deem no other scenes could e'er impart
Such wealth of happiness as seemed to come
In those long tramps through woods and fields at home;
To dote on every nook and pathway where
The wild flowers bloomed and fragrance filled the air;
To love each hill-top on whose magic height
Our roving footsteps climbed with new delight,
Till our young hearts leaped up with blissful bound
At all the pictured loveliness around;
To sigh for these dear scenes when forced away
And homesick pine thro' many a weary day,
Returning often bag and baggage home
When no one gave the kind permit to come?
Ay, call it weakness of a boyish heart;
It was a yearning which would ne'er depart
With boyhood's years,—a fondness which would cling
In later life, tho' time and change might bring
Their winter chill, and years of absence quell
The youthful ardor of its powerful spell;
A steadfast bond asserting its control,
A true attachment anchored in the soul.

Come hither, Muse! nor longer stop to dream;
The hour is flitting—gather up your theme
And bear it onward to a fitting close;
Let not your verse relapse to stolid prose.

These modern times are different from the old;
Improvements come with innovations bold,
And skill and craft and industry have wrought
Strange revolutions which the sires ne'er thought.

The manufacturer and the artisan,
The farmer, trader, the professional man,
Have long ignored the old-time ways and arts ;
And marvelous changes now in various parts
Have taken place, till the fair town has grown
A populous, indeed, a wealthy town.
The village here, once known as Chandler's Mills,
Lapped in the valley, flanked by ancient hills
On either hand, hath spread its borders wide,
And feels to-day almost a city's pride.
The mill stream winding from the lake above,
Is tasked full many a powerful wheel to move ;
And the steam engine brings its force to bear,
Screaming its shrill note on the startled air.
What would the settlers of the old time say
Could they stand here, on this centennial day,
And see the progress of an hundred years,
And hear the shouts, the pæans, and the cheers?
What would the veterans say? How would they gaze
Around in strange bewilderment, and raise
Their trembling hands and voices in surprise,
Till tears of joy should moisten their dim eyes !

Who are the men who've helped build up the town,
And laid of late their earthly burdens down ;
Whose generous hearts were with large love imbued,
Whose labors live, a legacy of good ;
Whose memory green is fondly cherished here,
Whose ashes sleep within the church-yard near?
They claim some mention at our hands to-day
We have a debt of gratitude to pay
Which this good town with all its wealth and pride
Can poorly pay, and ne'er can lay aside.

The white-haired *father who 'neath yonder roof
Preached words of life, enforced with many a proof,
Who by example and by precept taught,
And for long years in every good work wrought,
Did well his part for the dear town he loved
And closed a life of labors well-approved.

Another, too, yet in a different sphere,
With kindly impulse left his blessing here ;
O'er whose low grave the monumental stone
Was reared by grateful townsmen, as to one.
A benefactor genial, kind, and good ;
A man of culture, generously imbued
With native gifts of intellect and heart,
A keen, quick mind, most liberal to impart
Its stores of knowledge, brilliant, too, with wit
Whose ready shafts would like an arrow hit :
A master of the pen, who if to-day
He walked with us, would give his genius play
And bring to these festivities a cheer
None else could bring and hold each listening ear.
We'll let him rest 'neath his memorial stone,
Here where his life was spent and labor done.
And cherish long, whatever fortune comes,
The honored name of genial †Dr. Holmes.

'Tis time to stop.   In sooth, how short is time !
Yet time is long when drags a tedious rhyme.
Much must be left unsaid, full much unsung ;
Some random sheets shall here aside be flung,
And we will curb the headstrong, wayward Muse,
That flighty bird that warbles so profuse.

---

* Rev David Thurston, for nearly fifty years Congregational minister
in town.
† Dr. Ezekiel Holmes, a prominent citizen of Winthrop, who died there
February 9, 1865, then editor of The Maine Farmer

But this protracted stanza should not cease
And die away in these sweet times of peace
Without one earnest word—one loud halloo—
For Winthrop boys who with " the boys in blue,"
Struck the grim monster of secession down
And gave their laurels to the good old town.
The days are fresh before us, with the glare
Of gleaming bayonets and the wild blare
Of war's dread trumpet calling loud: " To arms !
Defend the country, save her flag from harms ! "
The fire enkindled, ah, how soon it burned !
The spirit of the ancient days returned,
And Winthrop boys, as promptly as of yore,
Were on the war-path, sword in hand, once more.
No boastful valor showy on parade,
But shrinking timid where the bullets played,
Marred their fair records.   On the field of strife
Full many bled and some surrendered life.
They speak to us on this centennial day
With words more eloquent than tongue can say,
And lay an offering on the altar here
Which this old town may well be proud to bear.

Farewell, the Muse !   This is indeed the last ;
But look ! what vision from the misty past
Is this that moves across our pathway now
With moderate pace, all cumbersome and slow ;
What lumbering wagon of the days of old ;
What old black horse whose years are all untold,
Whose head and tail and fetlocks all hang low,
Whose tattered harness, built an age ago,
Was made the strain of time's hard wear to stand ;
What gray, old man who drives with palsied hand,
And looks about with quite indifferent gaze
On all the folly of these modern days ;

Whose pride is with the past, who stops his team
In yonder street, and seems to sit and dream
And wonder what this motley crowd are at,
Gazing at him, his team, his coat, and hat,
As if the like were never seen before,
And were not stylish in the days of yore?
We know him now, tho' we were but a babe
When he was old—this same old * " Uncle Jabe,"
Welcome, old man, we'll grasp you by the hand !
You are the sole survivor in the land
Of those old veterans who did speed the plow
In this good town, near eighty years ago.
Thrice welcome now, for you have lived to see
This gala day, with your great country free,
And your old township prospering all the while
Beneath the bow of Heaven's approving smile :
A boon vouchsafed by Providence to few,
Therefore a welcome hand we reach to you !

Farewell the Muse, coy mistress of all song !
Farewell at last ; the end approached full long
At length is reached.   Enchantress, fare thee well !
Hushed be the echo of thy minstrel spell.
'Tis gone—our harp is on the willow bough :
The blue-eyed maid retiring, leaves us now,
And goes serenely through the welkin blue,
Waving to us, as we to all, adieu.

---

* Mr. Jabez Bacon, upwards of ninety years of age and the oldest inhabitant
of Winthrop at the time of the centennial celebration.

www.ingramcontent.com/pod-product-compliance
Lightning Source LLC
Chambersburg PA
CBHW032007060726
47497CB00017B/2357